TOM LEVEEN

Random House 🏠 New York

Library of Congress Cataloging-in-Publication Data
Leveen, Tom.
Party / Tom Leveen.—1st ed.
p. cm.
Summary: As eleven different high school students recount, in their own voices, events before, during, and after the same end-of-year party, the stories intersect and combine in unexpected ways.
ISBN 978-0-375-86436-0 (trade)—ISBN 978-0-375-96436-7 (lib. bdg.)—
ISBN 978-0-375-86392-9 (pbk.)—ISBN 978-0-375-86393-6 (mass pbk.)—
ISBN 978-0-375-89569-2 (e-book)
[1. Interpersonal relations—Fiction. 2. Self-perception—Fiction. 3. Parties—Fiction.
4. Family problems—Fiction.] I. Title.
PZ7.L57235Par 2010
[Fic]—dc22   2009017824

Printed in the United States of America
10 9 8 7 6 5 4 3
First Edition

FOR JOY; FOR MOM & DAD; FOR THE GUYS; AND FOR JENNIFER S.

CONTENTS

BECKETT   MORRIGAN
TOMMY BRENT DANIEL
AZIZE RYAN ANTHONY
JOSH   MAX   ASHLEY

BECKETT MORRIGAN
TOMMY BRENT DANIEL
AZIZE RYAN ANTHONY
JOSH MAX ASHLEY

I'M THE GIRL NOBODY KNOWS UNTIL SHE COMMITS SUICIDE.
Then suddenly everyone had a class with her.

You know the one I mean.

You don't pick on her, because you don't know she's there,
not really. She sits behind you in chemistry, or across the
room in Spanish. You've seen her naked in the locker room
after physical education—a contradiction in terms if ever
there was one—but you don't know what color her eyes are.

What her name is.

What grade she's in.

She's always been there, like the gum under your desk in
math class. And when you do bother to explore under there

1

with your fingers, the first thing you do upon contact is jerk back and say, *Ew!* And when that girl leaves, it doesn't matter, there's another one ready to take her place.

To be *That Girl Who*.

That Girl Who always reads comic books in the library during her free period or lunch. That Girl Who wears the long, flowy dresses and Rastafarian tam and peasant tops—except for that month freshman year when she wore a Tony Hawk T-shirt after seeing an absolutely spectacular X Games in San Diego with her best friend and her family. That Girl Who smiled at you once and who you maybe meant to smile back at, but couldn't find the time because you just got a text from a friend you were going to talk to three minutes later in the hall.

It's no big.

Girls like that are like that by choice. One way or another, we choose to blend in, keep our heads down, not cause a scene. Our individual reasons might vary a little from girl to girl, but the result is the same.

We're safe.

We avoid all the high school BS because the fact is, there are a lot bigger things going on outside those halls. Things that no one else knows about.

I know.

Like the girl who never participates in class? Goes to games or plays or dances or pep rallies? Or talks to anyone? Truth is, she doesn't have time. She has to—*had to*—get home to take care of her sick mother. No one knows she's living by herself now because her dad took off years ago and never exactly left a forwarding address, and she's scared that someday the school will find out and make her go into a foster home. That soon the money is going to run out, which means she'll have to drop out of school and work for minimum wage to try to pay rent. That her junior year in high school will have been her last.

These are the things no one else knows about.

Things no one else knows about me.

I miss my mom.

If she hadn't added my name to our little—stress *little*—bank account in January, the month before she died, I don't know what I would've done. I was sixteen by then and managed to take care of all the "arrangements," as the funeral director called it. I had her cremated and spread her ashes on Shoreline Beach and in the Pacific. That's what she would have wanted. There was no service, no funeral, no piles of ass-casseroles in the fridge brought by suitably sorrowful relatives and friends.

My mom was not like me. She was lively. "Free-spirited," my father would call her, while secretly screwing a viola player from Seattle. We lived alone together ever since Dad bailed on us, and that was fine with Mom. "I don't need a penis to raise my daughter," she said when she changed both our names back to her maiden name when I was twelve.

So other than an occasional visit from a nurse when we

could afford it those last couple of months, it was just us. Musicians, if you didn't know, generally don't make a lot of money. Jennifer M. & The Pasadena Theory never hit it big. Plus Mom stopped writing music during her first round of chemo, but her Gibson Epiphone acoustic and recording equipment were still in the little studio she'd built for herself. People still bought her albums, every once in a while—I knew because I'd gotten a couple of checks for like five bucks, royalty checks from this indie label she worked with. I knew any future royalties would go to me now. The people at the music company were among the few who knew her and knew she was gone. I didn't even tell the people who'd known us the longest. Ashley, or her family, or Anthony and his family. Because I suck.

I might have to sell all her gear soon. For the cash. I don't want to.

On Saturday evening, the night of the biggest party of the year, I walk to the nearby Santa Barbara Mission, where I sit alone in the chapel. I stare down at my woven bag, which is stuffed with everything I had planned to bring to the party, if I go—my change purse, my cell phone, my used copy of *Batman: Year One* in case I get bored, the key to my apartment; *everything*.

I know the old lady who runs the gift shop, and she lets me in without paying admission. I like to come here and sit in the back pew, looking at the statues of Jesus and the saints, and the tourists who snap away with their digital cameras and pretend to have some sense of reverence. A lot of them don't bother pretending, I've noticed.

That's okay. Jesus and the saints don't seem to mind. There's more important things to worry about. There's a war on, after all. And people dying of cancer. Jesus and the saints probably have their hands full.

If there's no one else in here, which happens maybe half the time, I talk to Mom. I don't know if she hears me or not. She never went to church, so I don't know if she's allowed here now.

"So there's this party tonight," I tell her now. The Mission is closing, and most of the tourists are already gone. Any minute the janitor, Carlos, is going to chase me out with his big dust mop, which he likes to do. He tries to act like he's all upset with me, but he can't not smile when he shakes the mop at me. I like Carlos. He's real. I know because he sees me.

"I don't know if I'm going to go," I tell her, out loud but quiet in case someone happens to walk in and think I'm a total nutjob. And maybe I am, sitting here and talking to my mother who died almost five months ago as if she's going to talk back to me, or make a Virgin Mary statue cry or something.

"I mean, I don't know any of them," I go on. "I know *of* them. I know their names and who they hang out with and what colleges they want to go to. I know Antho still wants to play for the Raiders even though I haven't talked to him since—whenever. But I don't really know them. I've never been to a party before, not really. I mean, I couldn't . . ."

I trail off. Mom knows why I couldn't.

I was too busy feeding her when she was too weak to do it herself. That and six dozen other chores you don't want to imagine, involving every possible fluid the human body can produce, in quantities you don't want to think about.

"I feel like I should just do it," I say. "Just go. Like, I should go *because* I don't know anyone. Just say hi or something. Or maybe goodbye. To someone."

I close my eyes. "I haven't been to a party since Ashley's birthday right after freshman year."

Ashley Dixon. I almost smile. We'd been friends since kindergarten, all the way until Mom got sick. Then Morrigan Lewis moved to town and I didn't see Ashley much after that. I'd watched them throughout sophomore year, jealous at first. Then, consumed by Mom's illness, I'd stopped keeping tabs on my old friend. Jealousy was a luxury for girls who didn't have to drive their mothers to the hospital for chemotherapy. After a few months, it was like I'd never known Ashley in the first place. The day Mom told me about her diagnosis, she also made me swear not to tell anyone.

"I'll be fine," she said, and back then, her voice was still strong and lovely. "We'll be fine."

"What about Ashley?" I'd asked her. "Or her mom and dad? Can't we—"

"No one, kiddo. Not even Bob and Dianne."

"Antho and Mike . . ."

"No, not the Lincolns either, sweetheart. No one. Promise me."

So I promised and I kept it. I hid the worst news of my life from my best friends.

I feel a pang of guilt, realizing this is the first time I've really thought of Ashley in more than a year, despite seeing her every day at school. She'd say hi, relentlessly, every day, while Morrigan would roll her eyes. But the last few months, I haven't even looked at her. And Antho, he's been looking distracted, and hasn't seemed to notice me slowly becoming invisible.

"Okay, I'll go to the party," I say to Mom. "If you really want me to. I'll go and I'll . . . I'll talk to someone. Ashley. Or someone. I'll make small talk. If you really think I should."

Mom, Jesus, and the saints are quiet.

When the Mission closes for the night—some other janitor who I can only call Not Carlos is the one closing up—I take a bus, a.k.a. the Loser Cruiser, toward the house where the party is being held, but I change my mind after the bus crosses State Street. I get off at Micheltorena to catch another bus back toward State. When I transfer buses, I have to pretend not to notice Morrigan Lewis screaming at me from across the street. Ashley is probably nearby and I don't want to run into either one of them.

I jump on the bus the instant it stops, telling Mom there's no way I'm going to this party.

• • •

I'm getting hungry, so I go into a pizza place on State, and I'm surprised to see that Azize works here. He's about the closest thing I can call to a friend, if by friend you mean someone I talk to once in a while in the library. Azize is cool. He reads good comics, anyway. I say hi to him, but then I realize I don't even have enough money on me to pay for a stupid slice of pizza, so I say goodbye and keep walking down State. How embarrassing.

I pass by Charles, who is this elderly African American man who plays violin on State Street almost every night. He's amazing. He plays everything from Mozart to Led Zeppelin. He's playing *Le Nozze di Figaro* as I walk past, and I stop to listen. Charles smiles at me, and I try to smile back, but I'm not in the mood. I like Charles. He's real. I know because he sees me. Charles's eyes sparkle under the streetlights, and he sashays over to me, like he's asking me to dance with him. That gets me to smile, and Charles's smile gets even bigger, showing off cracked teeth the same color as his gray hair.

"Like your hat, Sweetpea," Charles says as he plays and smiles away.

Charles's music is starting to get to me. It's inspiring in one sense, but also rubs my mood the wrong way. Like Charles is trying to cheer me up and I'm too immature to accept it.

That doesn't seem fair to him.

I scrounge in my bag. Charles deserves something for his trouble. All I can find is this handful of change that wouldn't buy so much as one slice of pizza. I can't afford to give it to him.

Then as I listen to him play and notice how empty his violin case is—there's a handful of loose change in it, no bills, just like my own purse—I realize he probably needs the money more than I do. First thing Monday morning, I'm on a job hunt, hopeful I can at least get hired as a barista or something, maybe at Coffee Cat. Maybe a second job too, if it comes to that. I've already sold Mom's old car to a used car dealership.

I drop my two quarters into Charles's case, which land in the spot where the scroll—or headstock if it was a guitar—would rest, then walk on down State before he can react. I don't need to stand there and make him feel like he has to say thank you, like I'm doing him this big favor.

I continue walking toward the Wharf. I follow the pier all the way to the end and dangle my legs off it, watching the ocean roll in and out, inhaling crisp air.

I decide that going to the party is, frankly, the dumbest idea I've ever had.

"They don't know who I am," I say, hoping Mom can hear me over the waves. "They probably won't let me in. I never joined a club or went to a play or a dance. This is stupid."

I bought a yearbook, once, last year, but never gave it to anyone to sign. Never even opened the thing. I forgot it in the library the day I bought it, and almost didn't bother to go back for it. Never had a boyfriend to write a heart over my picture or anything like that. One of the many drawbacks to being invisible—hard to go on dates.

The waves, uncaring, crash against the beach.

• • •

It took less than two years.

Less than two years for the illness to eat her, one bite at a time, chewing on my mother's breast, then wiping its mouth and moving on to the main course of liver. Mom was a fighter. Back and forth for months at a time, fighting the cancer, trying to keep her spirits up. I started reading *Batman* right when it began, alone—at first—in the school library. I named the cancer Joe Chill, after the character who killed Martha and Thomas Wayne. Fitting name for the monster who took my remaining family.

I knew she would lose. Mom had even had her liver transplanted. The survival odds were about 65 percent after five years if everything went well.

It hadn't gone well.

But Mom cried only once that I know of. Ever. I was feeding her soup when she burst into tears. I assumed at first it was the pain, or the anguish of the cancer.

"It's not right," Mom said. "You're so young, Beckett. You shouldn't be doing this. You should be out with your friends. Out having fun."

I don't have any friends anymore, I thought, but didn't say it.

"You should stay up all night," Mom said. "Watch the sun rise. From the beach. You should come home after dawn. So I can ground you. But you won't care. Because you had such a great night. It's not fair."

"It's okay," I said, but knew it wasn't. I knew exactly what my mother meant. My childhood was over. We should have been warring with each other, typical mother-daughter stuff, where I could scream *You don't understand!* and Mom would yell at me or ground me and I could slam my door and cry and listen to music and write dumb angsty poems in my empty velvet-covered journal.

I hadn't done any of that. I couldn't. I was busy. Dad had been the big moneymaker, bringer of bacon, before he left, and Mom was too proud to ask for help. She didn't ask me to help, either. I just had to.

The crying took too much energy, and Mom was sliding into exhausted sleep.

"Go to the beach," she slurred, chicken soup trickling out of the corner of her mouth. "Watch the sun rise. Beckett. Go . . ."

She fell asleep.

I cleaned her face with a damp washcloth and dumped the rest of the soup into the kitchen sink. Then I walked to my room, closed the door, knelt at the edge of my bed with a pillow stuffed against my face, and screamed, screamed, screamed.

Joe Chill only laughed.

I can't sit on the pier anymore, so I get up and wander off. Part of me knows where I'm headed, while the other part tells me not to do it. I do it anyway.

The tide is ebbing when I reach Shoreline Beach. The ocean is magnetic, tempting me to fling myself into the waves and float away, wherever the tide takes me. I won't do it, though, not really. I don't want to die. It's the absolute last thing I want. Seen enough of it up close.

But I still wonder if anyone would notice if I did.

I hunker and stare out at the water, debating the possibilities of the party. Out in the Pacific, a boat bobs on the waves, its white lights arcing back and forth as the boat cruises along. Behind me, a high cliff blocks any sound from the rest of the city, making this solitary spot on the beach my own domain.

It's one of the reasons I spread her ashes here.

All I have to do is walk up the steps behind me, to Shoreline Park, and up the street to the party. It's easy. I could just do it.

But why? I mean, what's the point? Some pointless exercise in validation? "Notice me, notice me, show me I'm alive!" Meet a guy, have a passionate romance during my non-senior senior year?

Ridiculous.

Even if there is a guy out there for me somewhere, I'll never know it.

This is dumb.

It's like I'm *already* dead. If a tree falls in the forest, does it make any sound? If a girl doesn't speak, if no one knows her name, does she really exist?

But I have to know. Does anyone know who I am anymore?

This becomes my new motivation: Go to the party. Walk around. See if anyone, just one person, says my name. Says "Hi!" Says "I had Spanish with you sophomore year."

If no one does . . . then case closed. My high school career, my existence, will be proven invisible.

I force myself up the stairs built into the cliff face, and down Beachfront to the party. I regret my decision the moment I open the door.

Later, I run up Beachfront, away from the party, and sit down on the curb and rest my arms on my knees.

Stay out all night? Watch the sun rise? Be with my friends?

Dreams. Ravings, really, from a half-dead woman succumbing to pain meds and disease. Why couldn't I have figured that out before I stepped foot in that dumb house?

I open my *Batman: Year One* book again to keep myself from crying. *Maybe it's all I deserve now,* I read on page one. *Maybe it's just my time in Hell.*

I hear ya, Lieutenant Gordon.

I struggle to read beneath the light of a streetlamp, and at first, I don't pay any attention to the sirens wailing in the distance. They are background noise to any city of moderate size like Santa Barbara. I do pay attention when three police cars and an ambulance turn onto Beachfront from Shoreline and park in front of the house where the party is still in full swing.

I wipe my face and watch two cops go toward the house. I'm too far away to see exactly where they go, but they're headed toward the front door. I see one of the paramedics wave over his partner farther down Beachfront, near the intersection with Shoreline.

Something's happened.

A minute later, two different cops head up the lawn. I stand up, shove my book in my bag, and start walking slowly back toward the house, drawn by morbid curiosity. Suddenly there's a flood of kids on the front lawn, not running but scattering all the same toward their cars or sitting on the sidewalk.

I walk until I can see the house in full view again. I wander up to a guy standing by himself near the sidewalk and ask him what happened.

I wonder if he knows what color my eyes are.

What grade I was going to be in.

What my name is.

BECKETT **MORRIGAN**
TOMMY BRENT DANIEL
AZIZE RYAN ANTHONY
JOSH MAX ASHLEY

TONIGHT IS THE BIGGEST PARTY OF THE YEAR, AND IF MY
DAD DOESN'T STOP YELLING, I'M GOING TO MISS IT.

This is so stupid.

What happened was, I just got my first car late last week for
my sixteenth birthday. An old powder-blue Super Beetle my
dad got from some car dealer friend of his. I had my license,
but only by a matter of days. I was still sort of learning to drive
the Beetle because it's a stick, but I'd *obviously passed the test* to
get the license in the first place, right?

So I told my mom I was going to this party, and she gave me
twenty bucks for food (more like five for food and fifteen for a
little pot, to be purchased on-site from this dude in the drama

department who was hosting the party, not that my mom knew that). Ashley and I spent all day today talking on the phone about what we were going to wear; who was going to be there; if we should smoke weed too or just drink; if you *had* to have sex with one guy, who would it be . . . the usual stuff.

(Answers: Black cargo shorts, red tank, red Chucks; *everyone* from school; drink first, smoke later; and this guy Ryan from my English class . . . I mean, if I *had* to. Ashley declined to "speculate on the latter.")

What I *told* my mom was, we were, and I quote, "going to this party." No big, right? What I guess I *should've* said is, "I'm driving to this party in my new (old) car."

My mistake, because:

About twenty minutes ago, I walked into the living room. There was a baseball game on. (There's always a game on, of some sort.) I stood in the doorway and said, and I quote, "I'm going to drive on over to Ashley's now." Who lives like three miles away.

My mother, deeply into her daily crossword puzzle, said: "Uh-huh . . ."

My father said: _____

Which is not unusual for either one of them. Unless I have spontaneously burst into flame, which only happened that once (just kidding!), I blend into the beige walls of my house as far as they are concerned. *Keep those grades up!* and *Don't you get pregnant!* are my only rules as far as I know. Outside of those, I do what I want. Which is cool. For the most part.

Case in point: Mom has no problem with me going to a party, or giving me money. So she's like all awesome, right?

Sure.

Since my mom had acknowledged my plan, I walked out to the old blue Super Beetle, got in, started her up, and began driving (slowly) over to Ashley's house to start getting ready for the party. It was already eight o'clock, and the party was supposed to have started at seven.

No kidding—two minutes later, my cell rang.

It was Mom.

"Where are you!" she screamed.

I seriously could not stop myself from laughing. I laughed out loud, and it was one of those laughs that starts with a sound like you're spitting milk out. *Ppppppptb, buh ha ha ha!*

Something like that.

I'm amazed she even noticed I was gone. Before I got a chance to tell her, "Uh, I'm like a block away," she screamed, "Get *back* here with that *car* right *now!*"

For a second, I thought something must be wrong with the car and Dad didn't tell me. It's not like I have to drive on the 101 to get to Ashley's or the party, but maybe the brakes are worn or something. Funny, you'd think he would have mentioned something like that, right?

So I said, "Uh, okay," and turned the car around. I wasn't laughing anymore. I got back to the house and went inside.

"What's wrong?" I asked as I went into the living room. Again.

"You put those keys on the table," my dad said. His eyes didn't leave the TV screen.

I set the keys down, functioning on autopilot because I swear to god, I was *so* confused.

"Ohhhh-kay," I said, and waited.

He didn't say anything. I had no idea where my mother was.

"So," I said, "what is it? What's wrong with the car?"

My dad: _____

I swear, you know? Say something! ₁

I tried again. "Dad . . . ?"

And that's when my mom came in. "There you are!" she shouted, and—again, I am unable to help myself—I started laughing.

"Glad you noticed!" I said back. "What's going on?"

"We told you not to take that car anywhere until you ask us first!" Mom declared.

I felt something in my head make a sound like this: *DOINK! Huh?*

So I said, "Huh?"

"Don't grunt, Morrigan, you sound like a caveman," Mom said, and plopped down on the couch again and picked up her crossword puzzle. Like, *This conversation is over.*

Which, I assure you, it was not.

"Wait, wait, wait," I said, and held up my hands. (And god, that television was on so *loud*! And they complain about my music, you know?) "I stood here like five minutes ago and told you I was going to Ashley's."

And here . . . here is where it all went south of heaven.

My mother said, and I quote: "You said no such thing."

Well. *Now* it's on.

"*Mom!* I stood right here and said 'I am driving to Ashley's,' to which you responded, and I quote, 'Uh' and 'Huh.' Which," I added, because I get a bit sarcastic when I get pissed, "when spoken together, is apparently *not* a grunt."

I didn't hide a grin. That was pretty good, if I said so myself.

Mom didn't agree. "Don't be smart, Morrigan."

I felt my eyebrows shoot up past my bangs. "It's what you said!"

"You don't raise your voice to us, young lady!" Dad snapped. And his eyes, I swear to god, have not, do not, and will not leave the TV screen.

Asshole.

"Well, could you please turn the TV down so you could hear me better?" I asked. Perhaps a shade too politely.

This earned a glance from my mother to my father, who did not glance back. Mom shrugged her eyebrows as if to say, *Well, you have a point, the TV was on really loud so maybe I didn't hear you correctly, and maybe since you're such a good kid I should give you the benefit of the doubt just this once so you can go to the biggest party of the year with your best friend.*

At least, that's what it looked like she was thinking. Then she filled in a word on her puzzle and the moment was gone.

I paused. I waited. I hesitated.

Then I flung my arms up in the air and turned for my room.

From the couch, Dad barked, "Where are you going?"

As if we were having a conversation and I'm walking out in

the middle of it. *Uh, except you stopped talking three minutes ago. Please tell me my parents are not the only ones this lame.*

I stopped. "To call Ashley and get a ride, I guess."

And he says, "You're not going anywhere."

By that point, I was literally shaking with rage. My hands were freezing and coated with sweat. I could kill them both.

"What?" I asked, just to clarify.

"You took the car without permission, you're staying home," my mother said, as if this made the most sense in the entire world.

And with that, I had officially *Had It.* I'd already driven the Beetle all by my responsible self, what the crap was up with this? Maybe it was only around the block, but *still.* Do I have to ask permission every time I need to drive somewhere until I'm eighteen? And I *did* ask—or *told,* anyway, and they didn't say no, which is pretty much the same thing.

So I bolted back into the living room and *unloaded.* I repeated my side of the story (a little loudly) and stood in front of the television, partly so they'd hear me and partly to piss off my dad. Well, the second part of the plan worked—he jumped up and started yelling at me about responsibility and my tone of voice.

So I shut up and folded my arms and pretended to listen.

This is hopeless.

He's been going on for about ten minutes now. It takes me about two of those ten to realize it's between games.

He's held it all in until the game ended. At least that's what it seems like.

The game comes back on, and the *asshole* doesn't even bother to trail off or fade to black. The moment, the very *instant* he hears an announcer's voice, he cuts himself off in the middle of a word. The word is *attitude,* but ends up being only *atti.* As in, *Morrigan, I've had it with your crappy atti.*

I decide I will spread this new word among my peer group. Yay!

Mom doesn't say anything, but I can see she agrees with Dad. Typical. She always rolls over for him. I've even confronted her about it in the past, asking her why it's always Dad's way or the highway, a phrase she's actually said to me. (Lame.) Mom only laughed and said I didn't know him the way she did. Is he like abusive or something? No, Mom said, still laughing, he's just who he is. Gotta love him, she said.

Maybe I have to, but I don't at the moment.

I can't believe this. I did absolutely nothing wrong, and now I'm out my car and a sweet night of partying with my best friend.

Once Dad's done, I go to my room and call Ashley. She knows right away something's up.

"What's the go?" she asks. It's this thing we say.

I tell her the entire story, and because she is my best friend in the entire world, she's ready to kneecap both of them.

"This *sucks!* God, Morrigan . . . what about the party?"

"I dunno. They said I had to stay home."

"Morry, no, absolutely not," Ashley says, like she has some sort of authority over the situation. "It's like the biggest party ever. We have to be there, celebrate with Antho and stuff!"

"I know, Ash." I sit on my bed and fall to the mattress, totally deflated. I stare at my black messenger bag, which is stuffed with everything I had planned to bring to her house— my change of clothes, a pint o' JD stolen from Dad's personal collection, gum, my driver's license (ahem!), Mom's twenty-spot; *everything.*

"You know what?" I say. "Screw it. Just come pick me up."

"Are you sure?" Ash doesn't sound like she thinks it's a good idea.

"Of course I'm sure, Ash! Call me when you're at the corner of the street. I'll be on the sidewalk by the time you pull up, and then I'm going to get in, and no matter what, you just *drive,* okay?"

My rage is turning to excitement. This is going to be fun. A total jailbreak. And there's a good chance my parents won't even notice. Once during a 49ers game, I told my dad I was pregnant just to see what would happen. The truth is, I've never had sex, because my stupid-ass ex-boyfriend got it into his wee stupid head that it would be wrong for some reason— like that's what God says or something. (Don't *even* get me started.) Anyway, Dad didn't respond until the next commercial, when he said, "Did you say you were having a baby?" And I said, "No, I said I have *rabies.*" And he kind of smiled uncertainly and turned back to the TV.

So I'm pretty sure I can bust out of here without attracting their attention.

Which, if you think about it, kinda sucks. What if some psycho broke into my room and kidnapped me? They wouldn't know until they got one of those ransom notes made from cutout magazine letters.

Maybe I should make one, just for laughs. But I remember a girl last year who called in an Amber Alert on herself, like she'd been kidnapped, so she could spend the night with her boyfriend. No way was I going to do something *that* stupid.

Ashley is a lot more cautious than I am. Which is probably a good thing. Her parents do pay attention to where she's going to be, who she's hanging with, that kind of thing. I'd never admit it, but it was kind of cool. Of course, we never did anything so bad that they'd bust her, even if she didn't tell them the truth.

Ashley's parents rock. I totally love them. And they totally love me. I spend as much time at her house as I can without being a pest. Her mom, Dianne, is a great cook, and even takes requests. (I love her baked pasta dinners.) My mom, on the other hand, orders in. Ashley's dad, Bob, always compliments our clothes. Ashley models new stuff for him whenever her mom takes her shopping. My dad? He frowns absently if I show off my belly, but doesn't comment. And they all hug each other, all the time. Even her older brother James hugs them. They don't exactly smother her or anything, but they, you know . . . *give a shit.*

Anyway—Ashley's caution comes through over the phone. She sighs and goes, "You know we were going to hang out all summer."

"I know. What's your point?"

"My point is, when you get home tonight—"

"Tomorrow," I interrupt, and laugh, because as this plan takes shape, I realize I'm going to have to milk it to be worth it. May as well stay out till dawn!

"When you do get home," Ashley goes on, "you are going to be grounded for like ten frickin' years, and then our summer is going to suck. You think about that?"

I shrug. Of course I haven't thought about it; I'm making this up as I go! And I tell her that, since she can't see the shrug.

Ashley sighs again. "All right, I'll do it if you want. But if you get grounded until school starts again, I'm beating you insensate with your own boots."

I grin. My best friend totally rocks. She's like my sister. If I had one. She was the first person I met when we moved to Santa Barbara two years ago, and we've been best friends ever since.

"Just call once when you're at the corner," I say, and hang up.

My heart is racing. I'm generally a *good girl*, in my opinion, but this whole car thing is *absurd* and unfair and it's not gonna keep me from this party. Plus, I'm kinda curious to see how long it's going to take them to figure out I'm gone. And now that I think about it . . . do I really want to know? I mean, what would happen if I came home at like six in the morning, and they had no idea? I think I'd be so pissed that I'd admit the whole thing just to see what they'd do.

I sling my bag over my shoulder, and check it one more time to make sure it's got everything I need. I feel like I'm about to break out of a juvie prison or something.

I listen through the closed door. The game is on. I can hear that much. Chances are good my mom is still sitting next to Dad, doing her stupid-ass crossword puzzle. To get to the front door and out to the street, I'll have to walk—or run— right past them. Their backs'll be to me, but the floor is hard-wood and squeaks, so sneaking past isn't possible.

I swear, it's like they installed it specifically to thwart me.

Will they try to stop me? Will Dad jump up and run after me and tackle me? No. He can't tear himself away from the TV. *He works so hard all week, Morrigan,* my mom says every weekend. Like that's some kind of excuse. I work hard too, more or less, at least during the school year, and you don't see me *potatoed* on the couch all damn weekend. Anyway, with any luck, Ash will pull up while the game is on and not during a commercial. During a commercial, he might be off the couch. If only there was some way to—

I turn. I smile.

I go over to my window, crank it open, and take off the screen. It's not a huge opening, but I'm kinda small, and I think I can squeeze through. I've never actually snuck out be-fore; I never really had to, not even when me and Josh were going out. But this'll buy me some time. And spare me getting tackled, just in case.

My phone rings once. I look at the screen.

Ashley.

I turn on my radio, not too loud or too quiet. A couple more seconds and I'm out the window, running like our friend Anthony, star receiver for SBHS, headed for a touchdown.

(*You like the analogy, Dad?*) I race through the backyard and out the gate near our driveway. My dad's polished blue Civic gives me a little cover from the living room windows. I hit the sidewalk as Ashley pulls up in her dad's beige car.

I fling the door open and leap in.

"Go, go, go!" I squeal, caught up in the moment.

Ashley doesn't peel out, though. She checks behind her for traffic, and slowly pulls back into the street. Such a drag.

"What's up?" I ask, a little breathless. I look back at the house, expecting my mom or dad to be racing after me. No such luck.

"Morrigan . . . ," Ash says, a little whiny, like she still thinks it's a bad idea.

I slap her thigh. "Forget it! We're free!"

"Where are we going? The party hasn't started probably."

"Not your place," I say. "As soon as they know I'm gone, that's the first place they'll call. Or look. We need to go somewhere else."

"Super Cuca's?"

"Oh, hell yeah!" I laugh. And finally, Ashley grins a little, too. Super Cuca's makes The. Best. Burritos. Ever.

"Your dad is going to freak out as soon as he finds out you're gone," Ashley says, turning onto Micheltorena.

"You know what? Screw him!" I say, and I surprise myself at how angry I sound. I guess I had more on my mind than just this junk with the car. "He won't notice, because he never notices anything! God, it might be tomorrow after*noon* before he notices."

Ashley chews on her lower lip for a sec. It's enough to tell me what I already know: that I'm right. Ashley's seen how my parents are. When she comes over and says hi to my dad, she usually gets a brief wave, or maybe a "Hey." They like her and all, I guess—or maybe they don't care who my best friend is. They acted the same way back in Rochester, before we moved to S.B. for "a better job opportunity" for my dad. (Clearly, this better opportunity consists of him muttering a lot and being absolutely useless on the weekends.)

"But they probably will figure it out sooner or later," Ashley says reasonably. "And then you're *done*."

"Ashley, can we seriously forget it? We're going to a *party*, you know? Can you not be a bummer, please?"

She pulls into the parking lot of Super Cuca's. We're lucky to find a space. Super Cuca's is a little shop with room for maybe four people at the counter, with a few tables outside on a patio. The parking lot is really tiny.

Ashley shuts off the engine and turns toward me.

"I'm sorry he's a jerk, Morry," she says. Her big blue eyes are sad and angry all at once, the way only your best friend's can be when she's defending you.

I squish down in the seat and fold my arms. "Not a jerk," I say, pouting a little. "Just . . . not there. He only notices stuff like, I got a D in English or yelled at Mom or something. Whatev."

"He ever notice the good stuff?"

I snort. I can do that in front of Ashley, it's okay. "Are you analyzing me now?"

"Just asking," Ashley says. "I mean . . . it's been two years and I've never seen him, like, hug you."

The last time my dad hugged me was when we put our cocker spaniel to sleep. I was twelve. Mom does it more often, these quick little squeezes in the morning if she hasn't gone to work when I get up for school, but usually she's already left for her office.

I remember one Christmas I had asked for this specific Barbie, and to be honest, I don't even remember which one anymore. But I know that I got it. And I was so happy. I ran over to my dad (sitting on that same damn couch, which we actually brought with us from New York) and jumped in his lap and hugged him around the neck and tried to kiss him. He moved his head. I tried again, and he moved again. I could feel one of his hands kind of tugging at the collar of my footie pajamas. Pulling me away from him.

I got the message. I climbed off him and said, "Thank you, Daddy," and he smiled and changed the channel with the remote. My mom smiled too, but kinda sad-like.

That sort of thing stays with you, you know? That must've been like ten years ago. A decade. It suddenly occurs to me I'm old enough to say *That was ten years ago.* Think about it.

But I don't tell Ash any of that. I don't tell her the only reason I think they're still together is me. Like they think they're doing me a favor by not getting a divorce. Sometimes I wonder. It's not like they hate each other, or fight a lot. They just . . . *aren't there.* At least if I got punished—grounded, or my mom slaps me, or my dad sells the car—they'll have seen me.

"On the other hand," Ashley says, interrupting my mental bitchfest, "maybe he doesn't know how."

"Huh?" I say, and think of my mom and cavemen.

"Maybe he doesn't know how to, like . . . tell you he loves you. Guys are like that."

Except he has told me that. A couple times, anyway. But I don't tell Ashley *that*, either. And yeah maybe guys don't know how to tell girls they love them; Josh *said* it all the time but would never *show* it, and I mean—

You know, who cares. The biggest party of the year is starting! Sitting in this parking lot bitching about my parents isn't how I want to spend what is probably going to be my last weekend out for a long time once they find out I've taken off.

If they find out.

"Hey," I say, and sit up in the seat. "Let's *eat*! We shouldn't get drunk on an empty stomach!"

"Oh yeah?" Ash says, and smirks. "Where'd you hear that, alky?"

"Uh, your brother-the-cop," I sass back. Ashley's brother James is a Santa Barbara cop, which is kind of funny because he was the one who first got us drunk, got us our first joint, and knocked a guy out once who grabbed Ashley's ass on the bus. That was all before he became one of S.B.'s finest, though. He used to play football for our school too with Anthony's older brother Mike. He was cool; so was Mike, and so is Anthony for that matter. I don't hate sports and I don't hate jocks—I just hate them on TV when I'm trying to, you know, *speak to my father*.

Ash cracks a smile. I can tell she's happy my mood's getting better.

"James starts his shift pretty soon," she says. "Can you imagine him arresting us?"

"Hell yes! He's *hot*!"

I say that from time to time to gross her out, which it does. She goes, "Ewwww, god!" and I laugh.

I throw open the door and jump out. I slam the door shut with a flourish. "Burritos and beer. What better way to spend a Saturday night."

Ashley laughs and we race each other to the entrance of Super Cuca's. I totally beat her. That's what she gets for wearing flip-flops.

The hell with my parents. You hear that, Mom? Dad? How's my *atti* now? Get bent.

I'm going to have a great night if it kills me.

So we order our burritos and take them outside, sitting across from each other at one of the tables for two along the patio wall. We unwrap our food, but then Ashley stops and squishes her eyebrows together (why's it called "knitting your brow," you ever wonder that?) and looks past Super Cuca's and to the intersection like she's checking something out. I turn around and look, too.

"What?" I ask her.

"Nothing," Ashley says, but then adds, "It's Beckett."

I sweep my eyes across the street, and it only takes a millisecond to pick Beckett Montgomery out of the scattered crowd waiting for the next bus down San Andreas. I'm white, like almost a ghost, but this girl's got my pastiness beat by a few shades. Only she wears this ridiculous, like, reggae hat thing that I have to say really looks out of place on her.

What a dork.

"Yeah, that's her, so what." I turn back to my burrito. I'm hungry after my jailbreak. Ashley and her used to be, and I quote, BFFs or whatever. They like practically *lived* together, hanging out with Antho's family for barbecues and things like that. Über wholesome, right? But they haven't talked since like freshman year. So who cares what she's doing now? Every day we passed her in the hall at school, Ash would say hi, and at first, Beckett would mumble something back. By the time the holidays had passed this past year, she stopped saying anything at all. Hello, freak show!

Ashley sort of frowns, and I'm like, *What the hell?* But I don't say it.

"She looks . . . ," Ashley starts, but doesn't finish.

"Like a Rastafarian? *Hey, mon.*" I snicker at my razor wit. What can I say—I'm a gem.

Ashley smiles a bit. "No," she says. "I was going to say lost."

I glance back at the girl as if I cared—which, it turns out, I do not. "She looks like she knows where she's going, Ash. C'mon, eat."

"Not *that* kind of lost." Ashley goes on unwrapping her burrito, but she's still watching her *ex*–best friend.

It's not that I'm jealous. More like . . . protective. The way Ashley tells it, one day they were friends and the next Beckett wouldn't talk to her much. Eventually they stopped talking altogether. (Don't blame me, it was before I showed up.) I'd seen her around school too, of course, but *chica* just kept her head down and her mouth shut, two things I'm not very good at. So how she and Ash ever got along I couldn't say.

"Didn't she like ditch you?" I say, just to make a point. "Go all like ice queen on you?"

Sometimes I do try to get Ashley to get pissed, because usually she's so laid-back and it amuses me, but tonight she's too smart to buy into it.

"I wouldn't put it that way," she says. "I just figured she met some guy or something."

"You kept calling her," I point out.

"Yeah, and she never called me back."

"Okay, so, who cares?"

"I guess I do, sometimes."

This is vintage Ashley. The girl just *can't not* care. About anyone. I guess it's one of the reasons I love her so much. I can be an unlovable little shit sometimes, I know. But I also know if I just stopped talking to her, she'd make it her business to track me down. According to her, that's what she did with Beckett, but Beckett kept brushing her off. Even an old soul like Ashley can take a hint after a while.

Plus we became friends just a couple months later. So like, I win.

But I'm feeling particularly *sassy* tonight, so I go, "Well, let's see what she's been up to," and stand up on my seat. I cup my hands to my mouth. *"BECKETT!"* I scream at the top of my lungs. The other patrons glare at me, and I savor the moment.

"Morrigan, what the hell!"

I give Ashley a shrug. "You want to know why she's lost, let's ask her."

Beckett's shoulders seize together in surprise and she whips around. She looks up, startled. This pleases me for some reason. I shout, *"C'MERE FOR A SEC!"*

"Morry! God! Sit down, dork!"

Beckett looks around, like she's not sure what she should do. She might not even recognize me, and she probably can't see Ashley behind me. Then she turns away, holding her bag close to her chest as the bus pulls up. Her long, dark, wispy skirt billows out behind her as she climbs the steps.

"Ooo, takin' the Shame Train," I say. "Poor kid."

I sit back down, grinning. I'm a bitch, I know it. But I'm so *good* at it. It's my spiritual gifting, as Virginal Joshua would say. Jerk. Straight-edge *queer*.

Anyway.

"What was *that?*" Ashley wants to know.

"It sounded like you wanted to talk to her."

"Well, maybe I do, but you just scared the crap out of her! It sounded like you were going to kick her ass, for god's sake."

"Oh, come on," I say, and take a big bite of my burrito. "I was just playing."

Ashley folds her arms on the table and squints at me. "Are you jealous of her?"

"*What?* God, whatev. No!" I swallow and pick bits of chicken out of my teeth with my tongue. Then I add, "Yes."

Ashley grins at me. "You're sweet."

"Why would you want to talk to such a bitch anyway?"

"Whoa, I never said she was—"

"No, *I* did."

"Yeah, I heard."

"So why?"

"She's not a bitch, Morry."

"What would you call me if I just stopped talking to you all of a sudden, huh?"

Ashley takes a drink of her soda. "Nothing. I'd just want to know why."

"Exactly, and if I didn't tell you, like ever, you'd say, to hell with that *bitch*, and move on."

"I did move on, dork."

"So why worry if she's 'lost' or whatever?"

"Oh my god! You really are jealous of her! I haven't talked to her in years, Mor. I'm just curious what happened. Her dad bailed on her a few years ago and—"

"Sounds lucky to me."

"Mor!"

"Well, maybe you can talk to her tonight," I say. "I'm sure she'll be there boozing it up with the Deaf and Mute Club or something."

Ashley tries to look mad, but laughs. "You are wicked."

Score one for me. I don't hate the *chica*, Beckett; I don't even know anything about her other than what Ashley says she used to be like. But I knew there was no way in hell she was going to this party. Way too shy. And possibly mental.

So yeah, I'm jealous. Ashley's the best thing that's happened to me since I got here, and I'm not going to let some weirdo Rasta chick ruin that. Best friends are hard to come by, you know?

"It's weird that she's taking the bus," Ashley says. "She usually takes her mom's car."

"Why don't you call her and ask her why?" I say, *slightly* exaggerating my excitement at the idea. It ticks me off that Ashley's been keeping close enough tabs to know what kind of car the freak show's been driving. "You still have her number in your cell, don't you?"

Ashley kind of sighs and doesn't respond. That makes me feel bad, so I let the topic drop and we both pick at our food.

I fish for another subject. "Antho coming?" I ask. That's what we call Anthony Lincoln. A lot of other people call him "A-train," which is frickin' ridiculous, but whatever. He and Ash go way back, like fourth grade, almost as far as her and Beckett, who's known Ash since like kindergarten.

Ashley shrugs. "I don't know. Would you?"

"Under the circumstances, probably not. But it's been a few months since, you know. Maybe a party's just what he needs."

"C'mon, Mor. Seriously."

"Okay, okay. I guess I'd stay home, too. But it's not like the football team's going to come to a party like this. I mean . . . are they?"

"I don't know."

I can tell she's getting bummed, and I can't let that happen, so I change the subject again.

"Speaking of *invitees,* do you think Ryan will be there?" I ask Ash with my mouth full. One of the benefits of eating with your best friend: table manners are not a big deal.

"Ryan *Brunner?*"

"Yeah."

"Oh, god, for real?" Ashley says. "I thought you were kidding about that. Are you out of your frickin' mind, Mor?"

I shrug innocently. "What?"

"Okay, rule number one, as everyone on the planet knows, is you do not hook up with your ex's friends."

"How is that *my* freakin' problem?"

Ashley gives me the big-eyed shocked routine. "It's been like a week since Josh!" she says. "Can't you at least let the sheets cool off? Geez, woman."

"They weren't that hot to begin with," I say, and take another huge bite of my burrito. I'd been trying to, quote, "watch my figure" ever since me and Josh hooked up six months ago. Not that I have much of a figure to watch; I weigh about a buck-five soaking wet, even when I'm wearing my favorite boots, and my pirate name would be something like Captain Lackboobs. Still, I did want to look nice for him. *Back then,* I mean. Well, screw that noise now, bucko.

"Sex is not everything," Ashley says, all grown up.

"But it is *something,*" I shoot back.

Ashley sets down her soda, still staring at me. She couldn't be more opposite from me if she tried: long hair, Southern California blond, beach tanned, blue-blue-*blue* eyes.

Me = short hair, brunette, pasty white, mud-puddle brown

eyes. And not only do we look a lot different, we aren't interested in the same types of guys. She went surfer/jock, I went punk. That probably saves us a lot of issues. No haggling over the guy stuff. Much as it *pains* me to admit, Josh is hot. Short, but hot. He's got this amazing black mop of hair that tends to curl over his eyes and just makes me—

Never mind. We're done.

"I'd take it back in a heartbeat," Ashley says with those blue-blue-*blue* eyes glaring at me. "How many times do I have to tell you that?"

"Todd loved you," I say, pointing a purple-polished fingernail at her. "You broke up with *him*."

"How do you know?"

"Because you told me, stupid."

"No, I mean, how do you know he loved me?"

"He must've, why else would you sleep with him?"

Ashley finally stops looking at me and shakes her head. "Morry . . . ," she goes.

And I'm like, "What?"

She takes another sip of soda. "We're sixteen years old," she says. "How the hell can either of us pretend like we know what love is? I mean, really, really know?"

"I know what it *isn't*," I say, and it's a lot bitchier than I'd meant.

"God, Morrigan . . . ," she says and shakes her head again. "You can't seriously be telling me that if Josh had slept with you, that by itself means he loved you."

"It's a good start."

A little physical intimacy never hurt anyone. Quite the opposite, I'd heard. A hug here, a kiss there. Too much to ask? Hell no. Couldn't get it from Josh, so fine, I'll look elsewhere, thanks much. I mean, we hugged and we sure as hell kissed, and we, you know, did quite a bit in the back of his Blazer, but if he wouldn't—

(Okay, for real, *enough*.)

"Is that why you wanted to do it?" Ash goes. "Because you love him? Seriously."

I swear, you know? Best friends are awesome, but sometimes . . .

"I cared about him," I say. "And I wanted to show him that."

"So there's no other way to do that."

"It's a *good start*."

"Did you know my parents never had sex?"

"So you're, what, adopted then?"

"I mean before they got married. I ever tell you that?"

"No. And, um, *ew*! Next topic."

"I haven't even told them about Todd yet."

Whoa. This is news. Bob and Dianne are like wicked cool. Ashley didn't talk to them the same way she talked to me, of course—I mean, what are best friends for? But they were in on most of her life, unlike two other parents who shall remain nameless. I never asked if she told them about Todd because I assumed she did.

"How come?" I ask.

"I don't know," Ashley says. "I just felt like they'd be disappointed. I mean, they waited, you know? So it's not like Josh is the only person on the planet who doesn't want to rush. But that's not why I wish I hadn't slept with Todd."

"Okay . . . ?"

"It's that . . . now I can't give it to anyone else, even if I wanted to."

"You can't have sex?"

"I mean no one else can be first. That's a big deal. Don't you think?"

What the hell does she know? Josh is a straight-edge religious freak nutjob prude, and that's the end of it as far as I'm concerned. And now Ashley's starting to sound just like him. Well, screw that. All I wanted was to know that he cared enough to be with me, and it turns out he didn't, just like everyone else in the world except Ashley. So screw him, and I don't mean in bed.

Plus, as we're sitting there in silence, our burritos getting cold, I decide it is way past time to change the subject again.

I cross my arms and lean back until my shoulders are against the wall of Super Cuca's.

"I don't want to talk about Josh anymore," I say.

"Why not?"

I look off to the right, turning away from the parking lot, and give Ashley my biggest, brightest smile.

"Because he just pulled up."

TOMMY

BECKETT MORRIGAN BRENT DANIEL AZIZE RYAN ANTHONY JOSH MAX ASHLEY

Josh and me were sitting on the sidewalk in front of Matt's house, leaning against the driver's-side door of Josh's dusty red '76 Blazer while I smoked. It was warm outside. The party was at a house near Shoreline Beach, so maybe if it got too hot, we could dive in the water for a bit.

Of course, if we did jump in the ocean, we might also ruin any buzz we had going at the time. All of us—me, Ryan, Daniel, and Matt—had been planning to get hammered at all costs ever since we got the party flyer on the last day of school. The plan was to meet here at Matt's, hang out for a while, then head over to the party and get good and drunk. Josh would drive, as usual, since he didn't drink. He's cool like that.

Then Josh showed up. His mood sorta ruined the evening, which sucked because usually it was his mood that got the party started even if he wasn't a drinker.

I looked over at him.

"So what do you want to do?"

"Fuckin' kill her," Josh spat.

I said, "Okay."

I finished my cigarette and we went back into Matt's house. Ryan and Daniel were playing Madden Football as Matt rummaged through his CDs. All trying to act like it was just another night out, when for Josh it was anything but. That first weekend without your girl is a bitch, I guess.

We needed to get him to the party, fast. Maybe even try to get a couple beers in him for once and spend the whole night ragging on his ex. Problem was it was still early; lots of time to kill. It was only eight-thirty.

Josh didn't say anything as we walked back into Matt's room. He went over to Matt's desk and slumped down in Matt's ratty old swivel chair. Matt gave me a look as if to say, *He feelin' any better?* I shook my head a little. Matt frowned and shut off this Jennifer M. & The Pasadena Theory CD—she had this voice that punched your guts but it was somehow not appropriate background noise—and traded it out for Minor Threat. Probably to try to cheer up Josh.

"You can't just be happy with what you got," Matt said suddenly in response to a lyric.

We all looked at him.

"It ain't possible," Matt went on. "Even if it was, it ain't practical. If you was just happy, like . . . like livin' each day like it was your last or something, you would't go to school, you wouldn't go to work. You'd just bang every babe you could."

He paused and took a breath. Looked around at everyone.

"Right?"

We all laughed at him, because that's what friends do. Matt took an appropriate moment to look pissed, then laughed with us, because that's what friends do, too. We didn't laugh too long, though, because the "bang every babe" comment had hit Josh hard, and none of us caught it until it was too late.

You could see Josh thinking, *Wish I'd thought of that.*

Morrigan and Josh had been going out for about five or six months. He was really into her, but not so into her we all got left behind. You know how that happens sometimes. I admit, we all pretty much liked her; she didn't seem to mind that he spent time with the guys, since she was permanently attached to her friend Ashley. The girls I'd dated inevitably got all pissy about me hanging with Josh or the guys, so I ended up breaking up with them because it was like, you can't tell me who my friends are, right?

Ryan, on the other hand, never broke up with anyone, because he never actually *dated* anyone. He just hooked up. He was one of those guys who could pick a girl out of a crowd, like a lion picks out a weak gazelle or whatever. Ryan hooked up like nobody's business, and I think the guys were a little jealous of him for it. He stayed away from the girls they liked or dated, though. Maybe it would have been better if he didn't. Josh never would have gone out with Morrigan if Ryan had been there first.

Thing is, Josh was a virgin, but we never gave him any grief about it. Well, almost never. He was cool with it. It was some half-religious, half-straight-edge thing with him, or at least that's how it sounded. So we gave him shit sometimes, because that's what friends do, but we also envied him somehow. Just a little. He never threw his guts up or woke up hacking green crap, for instance. So yeah, we were jealous of that.

At least we were until Morrigan tore his heart out. He didn't have the consolation of even having had sex with her.

So she had to die. I suggested we discuss how to kill Morrigan Lewis.

The topic got Josh talking again. Awesome. Daniel and Ryan even turned off their game.

"Dragging her behind the Blazer has a certain appeal," Josh said. "Or maybe just like a couple of baseball bats. Beat her ass like a piñata." He flexed his fists, his two black X tats squirming under the skin as if to get out and attack his ex.

"Antifreeze," Daniel suggested. "Slip it into her beer. That would be hard to trace back to anyone."

Josh nodded enthusiastically and flipped his bangs out of his face.

"Just shoot her," Matt stated. "Why get complicated? I mean . . ."

"Who's got a gun?" Josh asked.

None of us did.

"Plus then the news gets involved," Ryan pointed out. "If it bleeds, it leads."

We stared at him before laughing again. Ryan flipped us off and checked his cell for the time. He was probably ready to start drinking. And he was probably ready to start his prowl for a chick to spend the night with.

"You know what the problem is," Daniel said, "is that we're even talking about this. If you'd attacked her right when it went down, it would have been a crime of passion. Now it's premeditated. That's like first-degree murder or something."

I didn't mention we'd all be guilty of conspiracy, but whatever. Not that it mattered; it was all testosterone macho horseshit anyway.

"And hey . . . I didn't hear the whole story, Josh," Daniel added cautiously. "I mean, I know what happened, but . . ." He let the word hang. Daniel's the analyst of the group. He loves it when there's tension so he can dissect people's heads. He won't pick a fight, but if there's a conflict, he'll be there to pick it apart and study it.

Josh stared at the carpet. It was stained with three years' worth of Super Big Gulp soda and ashes from when we used to smoke in Matt's room. Evidence the room had been populated with high school guys, I guess.

No one said anything; the spotlight was Josh's, if he wanted it.

"I went to her house," he said.

None of us moved. Distraction could end the story. I could tell Ryan was struggling not to look at his cell for the time again, ready to get the story over so he could get "drinkin' and doin'," as he called it. The Minor Threat CD was still playing, like an outraged sound track to this monologue. Very cinematic or something.

"And she came outside," Josh said. "Said we needed to talk. I said okay. She asked me why we hadn't slept together, and I told her—I was like, because I don't think it's a good idea. And she's all, because of me? And I said no, that wasn't it at all. I just thought we should wait, that's all. It'd be worth it. We could do other stuff, you know? We *did* do other stuff. And then she's all, so you don't love me. And I'm like, no, that's not it. I just kinda feel like it would be wrong, you know, because, you know . . . that's what God *says,* and it's what I believe in anyway . . ."

I saw Ryan roll his eyes, but kind of behind his hand so Josh wouldn't see.

"And she goes, 'I don't care if God loves me, I care if you do.' Which if you think about it is pretty fu-cocked. And I said, I *don't* want to do it because I *do* love you. And she's like . . ."

Josh paused and shook his head.

"She said, 'you don't want to touch me.'" he went on. "And I told her that was dumb, I touched her all the time, but she just started shaking her head. And then she said it was over, and that if I couldn't show her I loved her, then there was no point."

"Is it the first time she's brought it up?" Daniel asked.

"Yeah," Josh said. "I thought she was happy."

He ran a hand back across his sloppy black hair.

"I guess that's what I get for trying to do the right thing," he muttered. He used a fingernail to pick at one of the X tats, like he was trying to scrape it off. I don't think he knew he was doing it. I wanted to stop him.

Was it the right thing? I mean, the rest of us had done it at least once, and it was no big thing. At least, I didn't think so. Josh was coming from a different place, and it's not that I looked down on him—it was his choice, and he's my bud, so I backed him up. He never told *us* not to get laid or drink or . . . whatever.

"So is she gonna be there tonight?" I asked. I was hoping not.

Josh shrugged again.

"Do you wish . . . ," Ryan started, then shrugged. "Nah."

"What?" Josh said. "Do I wish I would've done it with her?"

"Well, I'm just saying."

"No, Ryan, what are you saying?" Josh was getting pissed now.

Ryan must've felt the change in temperature. "No, nah, it's nothing," he said, and pulled out a cigarette.

"Whoa," Matt warned. Matt's mom was cool, but didn't let us smoke inside anymore, citing Matt's carpet as evidence. Fair enough. Ryan rolled his eyes, not hiding it this time, and shoved the smoke back into the pack.

Josh's hands kept clenching and unclenching. "Look," he said, like he was trying to stay all calm, "I know you guys think I'm like this total freak show for not having sex, with Morry or anyone else. But it's my choice, all right? No *babies,* no *diseases.*" He tossed that in Ryan's direction, since Ryan'd had more than one brush with both over the last couple years. Ryan just rolled his eyes again. I was happy when Matt punched him hard on the shoulder to make him stop; it was annoying.

"It's one thing I know I can get right, it's one thing I know I can control," Josh went on. "Me and her get together and that's fine, it's cool. Well, we *used to* get together. If she didn't like it, she shoulda just broken up with me, then she could go screw whoever she wanted! Which, it turns out, is exactly what she did, so no, I'm not sorry I didn't have sex with her. Especially not now."

The rest of us looked at each other. No one wanted to take the ball. Ryan looked a little guilty, but I could tell he wasn't about to open his mouth and make the night worse.

"I need a smoke," Matt announced.

It broke the moment, and we went out front again.

Outside, we all lit cigarettes, except Josh, of course. Him and me sat on the lowered tailgate of his Blazer. Matt sat on the roof, and Josh didn't seem to care. Daniel and Ryan stretched out their legs in the backseat. A few months ago, Josh had flipped the rear bench seat to face backward. "Tail-gunner," we called it.

"Well, soldiers, technically, it's senior year now," Daniel said, and blew a couple of smoke rings.

"Yeah," Matt said from above us. "Senior year. Dude, Josh, forget Morrigan! We're gonna be seniors. You can date whoever you want! Seriously, man. Forget her, I mean . . ."

"Totally," Ryan said. My guess was he was trying to make

up for what he'd said in Matt's room, to get Josh to feel better. Ryan hated it when people were mad at him. "In fact, you should get so hammered tonight, man. Just get blitzed for once. Forget all about her. That's what I'm doing."

"You're gonna forget all about Whore-igan?" I joked, which got a laugh. Nice.

"Man, I'm going to forget my own *name*," Ryan said, and we laughed again.

All of us but Josh.

I wanted to grab him and shake the crap out of him. Josh was the guy we all relied on to get us out of our own shit when it went down. He was the one whose house you could go to at three in the morning and wake him up so you could bitch about your parents or girlfriend or whatever. I knew because I'd done it more than once. I just liked hanging with him like that. Seeing him this way tonight was throwing us all off. I could tell I wasn't the only one who thought so. I hated Morrigan Lewis for doing this to him, and I hated her for what it was doing to *us*.

We'd been friends since junior high, us five. *Cinco amigos*. Band of the Hand (taken from this dumb eighties movie Matt loved). That sort of thing. Now at the top of our last summer together, it was going downhill because *Whore*-igan got it into her head to throw my buddy under a bus for choosing something that I'd have thought most girls would find—I don't know, noble or honorable or something. I just don't get women sometimes.

"Forget it," Josh said, and leaped off the tailgate. "I'm out."

He walked to the driver's-side door and fished his keys from his pocket. None of us moved. I wondered if he'd try driving off with us still splayed on his truck.

And I saw our whole night going down in flames.

"Josh," I said. "C'mon, we all gotta go party. If she's there, you can show her what a great time you're having without her, you know?"

Josh nodded; then the nod turned into a shake. "Naw, man" was all he said.

"What else you gonna do?" Matt asked him, looking like a modern-day gargoyle on top of a cathedral.

"Let's go get totally hammered!" Ryan cheered. "Rack up some sweet chicks and tear it up."

We ignored him. Josh spit on the street. "I'll prob'ly just go home," he said.

"What do you want *us* to do?" I asked, sort of squinting an eye at Josh. I didn't think it was a good idea for him to be alone all night.

Josh flipped his key ring around his finger, *jang-jang-jang.* "Call me in the morning," he said. "See if I'm still here."

The rest of us traded looks. Josh could have meant anything by that.

"Hey, man," I said. "If you don't go, we can't go. And we can't not go. C'mon."

"Exactly," Daniel said. "Someone's got to drive the getaway car after we poison her."

"Wait, what happened to shootin' her?" Matt demanded.

"Nobody's got a gun," Ryan reminded him.

"Oh. Yeah," Matt said, frowning. "Well, whatever we do, let's do it fast, 'cause I gotta eat."

We all looked at Josh, who was still flipping his key ring around in one hand, like he hadn't heard a word.

"Josh?" I said.

Josh shook his head. "Look," he said, gripping the key ring hard, "I don't think I can—"

Right then, Matt cut this magnificent fart, and we all laughed our asses off, rolling in the street. It was like a machine gun being fired underwater. It was an expulsion to be proud of, one for the history books. I knew we'd be telling stories about this epic Matt Fart ten years from now. He leaped off the roof of the Blazer like his ass had caught fire.

It saved the night from being shot to hell. He couldn't have timed it any better.

"Dude!" Ryan cried as we all scattered away from Matt, who was doubled up and laughing so hard he wasn't making a sound.

"Did your colon explode?" Daniel choked. We were all *dying*. Even Josh lost it, falling first against the Blazer, then collapsing in the street, like he hadn't had a good laugh in— well, at least a week, let's say.

After that, we all piled into the Blazer and didn't say another word about Morrigan. Whatever it was Josh *didn't think he could do*, he didn't bring it up again, and no one asked. I thought maybe I would, later, when things had settled down about Morrigan.

We headed out to Super Cuca's because Matt bitched again

that he was hungry, and one Super Cuca's burrito was enough to satisfy even him. Josh played Social D. on the Blazer's ancient tape deck, which meant he couldn't have been in too bad a mood.

As we rolled into the tiny parking lot of Super Cuca's, I noticed two girls sitting at one of the picnic tables outside the restaurant.

"Tommy . . . who is that?" Daniel asked me, real quiet, as Josh spent about three hours trying to maneuver the Blazer into an undersized parking spot. Me and Daniel were in the tailgunner seat.

Ashley Dixon. And Morrigan Lewis.

"Ah, *craptastic*," I whispered.

I knew Ashley from three years of English and knew Morrigan pretty much only as Ashley's best friend and Josh's girlfr—sorry, *ex*-girlfriend. I'd never had a class with her, but she stuck to Ashley the way gum sticks to your shoe. I wondered briefly if maybe the truth was they were some kind of *item*, which I guess would be kind of cool or whatever, but I didn't think it was true.

"Hey, Josh?" I said as he turned off the engine.

"Yeah," he said.

"You might wanna take a look, here."

"What." He cranked his neck around to look out the back window. Me and Daniel moved apart to give him a clear view.

The car was totally, completely silent. I don't think even another Matt Fart could have lightened the mood

I could see Josh's jaw clenching, his eyes not blinking as he stared out the window. We all waited. Ryan checked his cell, but otherwise, no one moved.

" 'Kay," Josh said. "So what."

"You want to wait here?" I asked. "Or we could go somewhere else."

"Right," Daniel said. "Let's just grab a burger or a pizza. There's this pizza place on State—"

"No," Josh said. He still hadn't blinked. "No. I live here, too. We're all going to the same school as usual in a few months, I can't avoid her forever." He opened his door. "Screw it," he said, and hopped out of the truck.

He walked—stalked—toward the entrance, shoulders thrown back. It would have been funny, really, because Josh is easily the smallest of the five of us, a full head shorter than me. Kind of stringy, but in a tone kind of way. And right then, he looked ready to swing at anyone who got in his way. Josh'd put in his time in some of L.A.'s most notorious mosh pits over the years, so he wasn't exactly scared of getting hurt, which can be a lot more dangerous than being someone who can hurt *you*, if you think about it.

"Oh, shit," the four of us said in unison, and scrambled to get out of the car.

We raced to catch up with Josh. I was ready to take a bullet for him, even if it would only be verbal. Morrigan was sitting at a table across from Ashley, her arms folded, and leaning against the wall behind her. She was maybe two feet from the entrance. She wasn't looking at us.

"What's up?" Josh barked at her as he got to the door. He

flung the door open and marched inside without waiting for a response. Good thing, I figured, because Morrigan didn't say a word.

I relaxed a little, but not much. At least he didn't start a fight right then and there.

Matt went ahead in, followed by Ryan. Daniel and me brought up the rear, but there wasn't room for all five of us at the counter, so Daniel was in the doorway and I was still mostly outside. Right near Morrigan and Ashley.

*Awk*ward . . .

I tried a smile at Ashley. She was wearing denim overalls over a black sports bra sort of thing, which did nothing for her figure but hung cute on her. Morrigan, as usual, had a punk/goth/emo sort of thing going on—*pothmo?* Whatever. She was cute too, with a narrow sort of face and short brown hair with bangs, but she was wearing this scowl that said *Talk to me and you'll burn in everlasting hell, got it?*

"What's up, Ash?" I asked as we jammed up in the restaurant door.

Ashley offered me knuckles, so I touched them with mine. "Hey, Tommy," she said, and smiled up at me. "What's the go?"

"What's the *what?*"

Morrigan snickered for whatever reason as Ashley grinned and said, "Nothing. What's going on?"

A good sign. At least she wasn't going to pull that girl crap where the best friend has to hate the best friends of the boyfriend. I hate that.

I glanced through the door. Matt had pushed himself to the front of the line, staring up at the menu; Josh had ended up behind him, looking at the floor; Ryan was talking with his hands, about getting drunk and who he was going to screw that night. Daniel, still half in/half out of the doorway, was keeping a cool eye on Ashley, sort of leaning against the door frame and trying to look badass.

I turned back to Ashley, shrugged, and jammed my hands into my shorts pockets. "Going to the party, I guess. You?"

"Oh yeah," Morrigan said, raising her soda like a toast.

Ashley grinned at her. "Morry's on a bit of a mission tonight," she said.

"Yeah?" I asked. "What's that?"

"Get fucked up and piss off my parents," Morrigan announced. "Or get pissed and fuck up my parents, whichev."

"That's a plan," I said.

Matt came barreling out of the shop with a greasy brown paper sack and a huge soda. "Dude!" he said to no one in particular, and ran to Josh's Blazer, where he dropped the tailgate and sat down. He tore the paper sack to shreds to get to his burrito. I didn't blame him. Super Cuca's is *that* good. And Matt is always *that* hungry. Food was way more important to him than any potential drama unfolding outside.

That's when I noticed Morrigan was looking over her shoulder through the window at one of the other guys inside.

"So you all going?" she asked, still looking over her shoulder.

I assumed she was spying on Josh, and said, "Yeah. We're all

going. Guess we'll see ya there." I shoved my way inside behind Daniel.

"See ya," the girls both said.

I bumped straight into Daniel, who laughed at me and said,
"Hey, settle down, soldier. The girls and beer will still be
there."

"Speaking of busty sex machines," Ryan said, flipping his
cell phone shut, "*I* am all hooked up, ya queers."

Man, I hate when he gets like that. Happily, Daniel shot
him down by saying, "I'm just so . . . stunned."

Ryan nodded, missing the joke, as Josh grabbed his paper
sack and squirreled toward the door. I body-checked him into
the wall just for laughs, which made Josh swear at me. Good.
He was still with us. I glanced at Morrigan through the window, hoping she'd see that he wasn't down and out, that he was
better off with me and the guys. She was paying attention, all
right. Just not to Josh. I didn't need him noticing she was going
out of her way to *not* look at him, so before he could make it
outside, I body-checked him again and started throwing rab-
bit punches. Josh fought right back, as usual, and lucky for
both of us wasn't in a bad enough mood to swing like he
meant it.

Morrigan didn't seem to care, but she was still looking
through the window.

I did the math, calculating angles, trajectory, factoring in
the Earth's gravitational pull with that certain magnetic
charisma some bastards are just born with, and came to
my conclusion.

She was checking out Ryan. Of course. Craptastic.

Ryan couldn't see her, though. "Bethany Carter, gentlemen," he said, stepping up to the counter.

"She's a tank," I said, glancing back through the window at Morrigan and Ashley, trying to predict what was going to happen once Josh made it outside. I still had him pinned against the wall, giving him slaps and punches to cheer him up while he cussed at me.

Ryan shrugged and ordered his food. "They all look alike in the dark," he said, looking pleased with himself. "Am I right? I am, aren't I. Color me *laid*."

Josh stopped trying to protect himself from me, and I let him go. His shoulders sort of slumped down, and he walked out.

Daniel turned to Ryan and whacked him upside the back of the head. "Dumbass," he said.

"Ah, hell. Sorry," Ryan said, and looked it. He did let his words get away from him from time to time.

"Now we'll have to cheer his ass back up," I said. "If he wants to go home now, it's your fault, Ry-o."

He dismissed me. "He'll be all right. We'll get him hammered and he'll forget all about his slag."

"Okay, one, you know he's not getting hammered. And two, what the hell's a slag?"

"Like a whore. In England. I think."

"Yeah? Speak American, jackass."

We got our food and started walking back to the truck. Josh hadn't made it that far. He was standing halfway between the Blazer and the table where the girls sat. Ashley's eyes were darting from him to Morrigan, like now she was the one ready to jump in front of a bullet. So I stopped too just to see where things were headed. Ryan and Daniel kept on going toward the truck, but cast glances back. Ryan even slapped Josh on the shoulder, trying to get him to move, but Josh was paralyzed.

The paper sack in Josh's fist crinkled as he tightened his grip on it. Then he turned and went straight up to Morrigan.

Here we go, I thought, and tensed. Even though Josh knew how to take it and dish it in a pit, he wasn't a violent guy. But under the circumstances, he might've been capable of anything.

"You going to the party?" he said to Morrigan.

Morrigan was giving him her profile, looking past Ashley into the darkness beyond Super Cuca's patio. "Sure. *You?*" She took a lazy sip from her soda.

"Of course," Josh said back. "Wouldn't miss it."

"Great," Morrigan said sarcastically, which was pretty normal for her. "See you there."

Josh nodded, staring.

Let's go, Josh, I thought. *C'mon, let's go.*

"You think maybe we can talk later?" Josh said, and I thought, *Oh no.*

Morrigan turned to him, her eyes slitted and pissed. "About what? *Jesus?*"

Josh clenched his jaw again and dropped his eyes. "No," he said, and I could see how hard he was struggling not to lose his cool. "Us."

"There is no us."

"Please?"

"Josh," I said, trying to rescue him. "C'mon, let's go."

Morrigan didn't say anything. Josh studied her, then added, "Will you at least think about it?"

"Sure, whatev."

Josh nodded again and finally turned to go back to the truck. I gave him a slap on the back as he passed me, but I had one more thing to do before we took off. I waited until he jumped in the driver's seat and slammed the door shut behind him.

"Hey, Morrigan," I said, and leaned close to her.

"What."

"Look," I said quietly, "I don't get the whole God thing with Josh either, okay? Nobody does. But you already broke up with him, okay? Don't drag him along."

"Hey, asshole, he came up to me!"

"Okay, I think—" Ashley said, and started to get up.

"I *am* an asshole," I said back to Morrigan. "Because what I'm asking you to do is not talk to him tonight. I know he'll try, and he might keep trying, but don't do it. He'll get over it. Don't indulge him or whatever. Okay?"

"Gladly!"

I straightened up. "You know," I said, "I'm glad you ended it. You don't deserve him. Think about that."

"Oh, I'll be up *nights.*"

I just laughed, to make her think she wasn't getting to me, which was not true at all. I'm kind of surprised Josh didn't take a swing even if it would have been jacked up to hit a girl.

"Parting thought," I said. "Go fuck yourself." I turned to Ashley. "Sorry."

Ashley sort of shrugged her eyebrows. I turned and headed back to the Blazer.

"Might as well!" Morrigan shouted after me. " 'Cause God knows he wouldn't!"

Whatever.

I climbed into the tailgunner seat beside Matt. Josh revved the engine and I thought he'd try peeling out of the parking lot, but he didn't. He drove all casual back onto the street and headed out.

Josh cranked the Social D. back up, which was good. We ate in the car as Josh drove, taking his own sweet time. At first I thought it was because he wasn't in any hurry to meet Morrigan again at the party, then I decided it was because he wanted her to get there first, for whatever reason. Maybe so he could make an entrance of some sort.

Damn, man. Relationships. You know?

We stopped for gas and then again for cigarettes because we forgot to get them at the gas station, screwing around and punching each other and stuff, trying to erase the showdown at Super Cuca's from the evening's memory. Ryan kept going off about how drunk he was going to get and that Bethany Carter could suck the chrome off a bumper, and that he was happy to recommend us to her when he was done with her. But there was still a sort of silence in the car. Maybe *heaviness* is a better word.

"Man, I hope this doesn't suck," I said quietly to Matt as Josh tried to find the house where the party was.

"Yeah," Matt agreed.

"Think she'll still come?"

"Morrigan?"

"Yeah."

Matt shrugged. "Maybe. Dunno."

"We're gonna have to keep an eye on him," I said.

Matt looked over his shoulder at Josh. "I'll do it," he said.

"You sure? I don't mind."

"Nah," Matt said. "I got it. I don't feel like drinkin' tonight anyway."

"Liar."

"Well, yeah, but I mean . . ." He shrugged.

Well, we'd need one of us four sober to keep Josh from *actually* killing Morrigan if she showed up. Our conversation about her murder was all BS guy talk, but I knew that when a guy gets his heart torn in half, he's capable of doing a lot of stupid things. And after the way she talked to him tonight, he could snap. Anyone could.

"For real?" I asked Matt. "It's a party, man."

"S'cool," Matt said. "I got his back. But if I run outta smokes, I'm bummin' off you guys."

"That's a deal," I said, and sank down in the seat.

It was good to know that when things got bad, someone would be there to back you up.

Because that's what friends do.

BRENT

BECKETT MORRIGAN
TOMMY DANIEL
AZIZE RYAN ANTHONY
JOSH MAX ASHLEY

MAX AND ME STOPPED AT THE COFFEE CAT AROUND NINE, WHICH WAS OUR FAVORITE PLACE IN JUST ABOUT THE WHOLE WORLD BESIDES THE BEACH, THE BEACH SKATE PARK, AND THIS BURRITO PLACE ON MICHELTORENA AND SAN ANDREAS. Max had filled his Lucky 13! card, which meant he got his thirteenth cup of coffee free, so he was all jazzed 'n' shit, which meant I'd be hearing about his good luck the rest of the night, or until we were both drunk, whichever came first.

"It's not luck," I told him as we walked down Anamapu to State Street, holding our boards by the trucks. "You bought twelve coffees, and the thirteenth was free."

"You're missin' the point, Brent. It's that . . . I got my Lucky Thirteen *tonight!*"

"So what's lucky about tonight?" I asked him, but not in a way that made it sound like I cared. Mostly I was checking out the sidewalk and street to see if there was any room for us to skate. We coulda, but it woulda been in an asshole kind of way, and I didn't feel like dealing with any tourists getting all bent out of shape. Saturday night on State is all crowded. We shoulda taken De la Vina instead of State.

"Tonight's the night," Max said, all serious 'n' shit.

"Tonight's the night for what?"

"HER," Max said, like it was all in capital letters.

I stopped in the middle of the sidewalk and laughed at him. I knew who he was talking about because there were only about four things Max and me ever talked about: video games, football, the X Games, and Beckett f'ing Montgomery.

Beckett was this hippie chick I had third hour with last year. She always wore long, flowy dresses, sandals, and these . . . whaddya call 'em . . . pirate shirts? Peasant tops? Some hippie thing. I always recognized her by the hat she wore: this knitted deal, green, yellow, and red striped. Which was weird, 'cause the girl was white as hell but the hat made her look like some reggae dude. I'd seen her in the library at school sometimes, all hunched over and reading comic books. *Comic books,* dude. What the hell?

Max'd only shared a class with her once, back in sophomore year: biology, second period, first row, second desk in.

Guess how I knew all that.

Since Max had never once talked to her, I didn't see why tonight would be any different. He'd followed her from a distance for the last three years and never, not even by accident, talked to her.

He did sign her yearbook once: our junior year, her sophomore. And that was only because she'd left it on a table in the library and he'd grabbed it real quick, then put it back before she came looking for it. *Mi amigo valiente*, right?

Max'd seen too many movies where a smooth dude can sweep some chick off her feet with a cocky joke of some sort. Max wasn't cocky, or smooth. He was just this big dopey skater who'd gone out for football sophomore year but didn't care enough to bother when he made the team. He coulda been like a linebacker or something, maybe gone to State if Anthony "A-train" Lincoln hadn't blown the last five games of the season. Max had no, what my dad would call, follow-through. And he'd never *follow through* with this plan of his, but he'd ruin the whole night talking about it if I didn't shut him down.

"Well, let me know how that works out for you, bro," I said, and we kept hoofing it to the house where the party was. My mom was using the car, and Max's folks were both out of town. No big. We both preferred skating most of the time anyway. That was one reason we hung out so much. Max was a monster on a half-pipe, which kinda pissed me off.

"You don't think I can do it?" Max looked all cranky-ass.

"Uh, no. You had your chance, dude. Three years of it."

"Bro," Max said, but I cut him off.

"Let's get some food," I said, and took a sharp right into a little pizza joint. It smelled awesome and I was ready to feed.

The distraction worked. Max followed me in and we stood there looking at a menu. Some Arab kid was behind the counter, and he smiled all big 'n' shit when we walked in.

"Hello!" he said, like all happy or at least pretending real good.

"What's up?" I said, but didn't really look at him.

"What can I get for you?" he said. 'Cause of his accent from like Syria or wherever, it sounded like there was a *d* on the end of his *r*'s: "fo-d you."

"Gimme, uh . . . a slice of that Monster Meat deal thing."

He punched it into the register. "Fo-d you?" he asked Max.

"Just a cheese slice," Max said.

"Veddy good," the kid said. "Fou-d sixteen."

We paid cash, and I watched him run the register. Not a lotta kids from the Middle East around here, and he looked familiar. His name tag said AZIZE, but I couldn't tell you how to say it. Also, I didn't much care.

"Hey, do you go to Santa Barbara High School?" I asked the kid.

He smiled again, all big white teeth. "Yes," he said. "I will be a senior next year."

"Oh," I said. "We just graduated."

"Congratulations!"

I smirked at him. *Congratulations?* Kinda a stupid word when you hear a kid say it.

"You are going to the party tonight, then?" he said.

"Uh . . . yeah. *You* going?"

"I am!"

"Oh. Cool. Hey, can I ask you something?"

The kid nodded. What the hell's he so *happy* about? He had this dork-ass white uniform on and was prolly making, what, nine bucks an hour? Nothing to smile about.

I leaned my board against the counter. "Are you like allowed to drink?"

His big smile dropped a little.

"I'm sorry?" he said, but it came out *soddy*.

"I said are you allowed to drink? You know, beer. Whatever. Isn't it against your religion?"

I only knew that from movies, so I wanted to see if it was true. There were a few kids at school who said they were Mormon, but that didn't stop 'em from getting plowed, and other kids who went to church but smoked and drank and cussed and screwed.

"I was not planning on it," the kid said.

"Oh," I said back. "So why are you going to a party then?"

"Dude," Max said, like I was giving this kid a hard time, which obviously I wasn't. I just wanted to know. Plus, come on, we just *graduated*. It was like a chance to hassle a freshman when we started sophomore year. It's just how things go. Life in America, man.

"There is someone there I would like to see," the kid said. He wasn't smiling anymore.

"Oh, hey, a hookup!" I said. "She hot?"

"Brent, man," Max said, and punched my shoulder.

"What, I'm just asking! So, is she? Anyone we know?"

"It's not a hookup," the kid said, and it sounded like *who-k up*, which kinda made me laugh. I couldn't help it.

"Brent, shut up," Max said.

"Okay, okay. Just messing with the guy. We're cool, right?"

He met my eyes evenly. Kid couldn't take a joke.

"We are cool."

Kew-el.

Funny stuff, that's all I'm saying.

So I left the kid alone and we got our pizza. Max immediately headed back outside, so I followed him. By the way, I also left a nice tip, and I told Max that once we were back on the sidewalk. I don't think he heard me.

We ate as we walked, after tossing our paper plates in the trash right outside the pizza place. It took us about ten seconds to scarf the slices.

We were walking past this old black guy who played violin every night on State Street, and I flipped a couple quarters into his open violin case. He nodded and smiled without missing a beat of his song. I don't care much about classical music 'n' shit, but that guy was awesome. I think he was playing Mozart or something. He wasn't having a very good night. There were two quarters shining in the red plush interior near the head of the case, and some other loose change in the body, but that was all.

"So you don't think I can talk to her?" Max said suddenly.

Here we go again!

"No, I don't."

Max looked all hurt and I almost laughed right in his face.

"You don't know!" he shouted.

I stopped walking. Max stopped, too.

"Yes, I do too!" I yelled back at him. "Bro, you have *never* talked to her! You spent the last three years talking *about* her but never *to* her! How the hell you think tonight's gonna be any different? And she don't talk, anyway. To anyone. Why would she even show? Dude, we *graduated,* man! Move on!"

"That's why tonight's gonna be diff'rent!" Max shouted back.

"Because you have nothing to lose?"

"Yeah!"

"Desperation," I said. "What a motivator."

Max pulled out his Lucky 13! card and shook it in my face. "This's a sign," he said. "My luck's gonna change."

"It's not luck, that's my point! It's about you growin' the *cojones* that you have failed to grow over the course of our high school career. You bought twelve cups of coffee and got the thirteenth free. That's not luck, it's a choice. You chose to buy those coffees. Well, you chose not to talk to Beckett Montgomery for the last three years. If you talk to her tonight, it's not because you got lucky—ha! Get it? Got lucky?"

"Bro" was all Max said.

"Look, what do you even see in her?" I asked him. "Is it the hat? 'Cause she's not even *black,* I don't know if you've noticed that. She's the opposite of black. She's *pasty.* How do you get that pale living in SoCal?"

"Dude," Max said.

"Serious, what is it about her? 'Cause that hat, man. For real. Like she's all Rastafarian. What's up with that?"

"Man . . . ," Max said.

"It ain't luck," I said.

I could see he was chewing on it. I looked aimlessly around State so I wasn't staring at him while he thought. The violin guy was laughing now as he played. I wondered if it was because of us. We weren't being quiet.

"I guess I see what you're sayin'," Max said, all slow, like he was still thinking real hard. "But what *I'm* sayin' is that I didn't get my Lucky Thirteen last night, or tomorrow. I got it tonight. That *means* somethin'."

I was starting to get pissed. Tonight was our last night of high school, for real. Graduation was cool and whatever, but pretty much anyone who was anyone would be at this party, and it was prolly gonna be the last time we ever saw them. Graduation was the ceremony; this was like the going-away party. I wanted to chug some brew and maybe see if I could snag a chick, and not talk about Beckett f'ing Montgomery all night.

"What're you gonna do? Give her a piggyback ride to your house? You got no car, man. How douche is that?"

"My *house?*" Max said, and his voice squeaked. "I never said anything about—dude, I'm not tryin' to sleep with her. That's not what this's about."

"You don't want to sleep with her?"

"No, I—I mean, yeah, of course I . . . I just mean, not tonight, that's not the point, that's not what this's about."

"What's it about then? *Luuuve?*"

"Maybe!"

"Yeah, or, uh—lust?"

"Of course there's lust!" Max exploded. "Yes, I want to do her! She's totally hot! But not tonight! I wanna get to know her, I wanna know everything about her, I wanna know who she is. I wanna hold her hand and take her to dinner and talk all night long...you know? And...yeah, I like her hat. So what?"

"You're sad, man."

Max looked really bummed, and I felt bad. I knew what he meant, of course I did. But for all the talking he'd done about Beckett Montgomery, he'd never said *that*. So this wasn't your usual hard-on for a babe in bio class. This was like magnetism or something. Which made this situation a lot more dangerous. Like yesterday—I'd heard about this girl Morrigan who'd broken up with her boyfriend because he was like some religious whack-job. I didn't really know either of them, so it wasn't a big deal to me. But I'd heard Morrigan's boyfriend was like totally devoted to her, talked about her the way Max just talked about Beckett. It's bad news if you think she's your soul mate, whether she is or not. I didn't want to see Max go through something like that. I mean, he's my bro.

I tried to think of something to cheer him back up. He was still looking all bummed out.

"How do you even know she'll be there?" I asked, trying to sound all reasonable 'n' shit.

"She will," Max said. "I know she will. If that pizza guy is going, then why not her?"

"Man, we've been to parties," I reminded him. "Never seen her. Never seen her at anything that had to do with school. She walks in on the last bell, leaves school right after last bell. She's like mental or something. You know? How do you know she hasn't joined the Peace Corps or something?"

"I dunno," Max said. "I just got a feelin' is all."

"Because of a free coffee."

"Because . . . I dunno, because it's my last chance."

"Ya'll go get that girl, son," the old black guy said.

Max and me both turned. The guy was kinda grinning, not looking at us, playing his violin.

"Was he talkin' to me?" Max whispered.

I shrugged. Couldn't care less. "Let's go," I said, and we kept walking down State. I think the old black guy was laughing again.

We walked and didn't talk. I wanted to skate so bad. This walking crap was getting old.

"You think I'm like a total freak?" Max asked suddenly.

"Totally."

"Serious, dude."

"No, not totally. If you'd been all stalking her or something, then, yeah. But you did keep your distance. That's good."

"I *dated*," Max said.

"Yeah, but you were thinkin' about her the whole time. That one chick, what's her name. Ashley . . . something."

"Dixon."

"Yeah, man, her. Dude, she was totally sweet for you and she was really hot and you totally blew her off. 'Member that?"

"Yeah . . ."

"You blew her off because you told me you were gonna ask Beckett to prom. And did you? No. So that Ashley chick went out with that douche surfer Todd before he bailed for Baja. You blew all *kinds* of opportunities because of this chick, man." Like screwing Ashley, which I heard Todd did, but I didn't bother bringing it up to Max.

"I know . . . ," he said.

"But," I added, "like I said, at least you weren't a stalker. So if you did talk to her, tonight, *finally*, at least she wouldn't like pepper-spray you or anything."

"Yeah?"

"Sure. But since we're on the subject—again—why the hell didn't you talk to her all these years? I mean, for real?"

" 'Cause she's awesome. And I'm . . ."

I gestured for him to go on.

"I dunno," he said.

"How do you know she's so awesome, since you never talked to her?"

"I guess I don't," Max said. "But I gotta find out. Look, I know you're right. I wasted all of high school starin' at Beckett and thinkin' about her and whatever. I know that. That's why I have to do it tonight. I have to know, one way or another, if there's even a chance."

"Okay, yeah, I get it, but look, man," I said, "you gotta understand something. I'm going to this party because I want to celebrate getting the hell outta high school. And that's what I'm going to do. I'm not hanging out all night listening

71

to you go off about this chick again. You know what I'm saying?"

"Yeah, yeah, that's cool, man."

"You sure? 'Cause I'll bail on you, I swear to god."

He actually laughed. "Naw, man. It's cool. You're right, I gotta grow a pair and just do this."

"Cool. Now, since we're on such a unique topic, can I ask you something?"

"Yeah, man."

"What do you really think is going to happen? I mean—like, what's your best- and worst-case scenario right now? Assuming she's there?"

Max didn't say anything for a minute. The crowded sidewalk had cleared a bit and I was itching to get on my board, but it woulda been hard to hear each other. Since I'd just asked the guy a question, it seemed dickheadish to start skating.

"Worst-case scenario is, I tell her I'd like to go out with her sometime and she shoots me down," Max said, trying to sound all calm about the idea. "Best-case scenario is . . . who knows, man? Maybe we get married someday."

"Bro, you are eighteen years old."

"I don't mean tomorrow, dude."

"Just checking. Hey, you ready to skate?"

"Yeah, let's go."

We dropped our boards to the pavement and got ready to roll. Finally!

And right then, I swear to god, who did we see walking down State under the 101 bridge?

Beckett f'ing Montgomery.

God*dammit.*

Max sucked in this big breath and damn near spilled his coffee. He grabbed my arm all melodramatic 'n' shit.

"Brent!"

"Yeah man, I see her," I said, and shook my head. I also pulled my arm away from him. It was too gay. Max was standing there, eyes all wide.

"See where she's goin'?" Max said, sounding all excited again.

"The beach," I said. Like, duh. The wharf was another couple blocks or so from the 101 underpass where Beckett's funky hat was starting to disappear downhill.

"Naw, toward the party!"

"Max, man, we're miles away from the party, she could be going anywhere," I said. "Plus," I added, and checked my cell for the time, "it's like nine o'clock and no one's gonna get there till like ten."

"It started at seven."

"What douche is gonna show up at seven? The drama fags?" The party was at this guy's house near Shoreline, some hot-shit from the drama department. Not my crowd, but I heard the chicks put out and the guys scored excellent pot.

"She's goin' to that party," Max said. "I'm tellin' you."

He started walking real quick. I had to jog to catch up with him.

"What are you doing?"

"Growin' a pair!"

"What, now?" I yelled as we kept jogging.

"It's what you said to do!"

I grabbed him. We skidded to a halt. I turned him around to face me.

"You can't just walk up to her on the street," I said. "She'll freak out."

"Well, whaddya want me to do, huh? You just said she *wouldn't* freak out!"

Okay. I had to help a brother out. "Look, let's say you're right, that she's going to the party. Cool. You want to talk to her there because it's your lucky night, cool. At least it's not outside the realm of, like, *expectation*. You jump on her on the street, she's just gonna get flipped out. Know what I'm saying? Then you *will* look like a stalker. At the party, it's like an organized event. You're *expected* to talk to a lot of people. Don't go picking up on her on *State Street*."

Max chewed on his lip for a second as he watched Beckett disappear under the overpass. Max and me called it Michelle's Hill, after this chick we used to hang out with freshman year who Rollerbladed down it once and totally jacked herself up when a rock lodged in her wheels. I mean, it was an epic bail, bad enough to get the hill named after her. Michelle moved to Phoenix a couple months later, still in two casts. Funny shit.

Max's board twitched in his hand, like he was itching to jump on it and cruise down Michelle's Hill to cut Beckett off.

"If you want to go, go," I said, all like exasperated. "But I'm going to the party."

But I didn't take off, and I'm sure he knew I wouldn't, because he still stood there, staring at the overpass.

"All right," Max said. "You're right. I'll wait."

"You sure?" I said, mostly to be a dick.

"Yeah," Max said, missing the joke. "Let's just head out."

"Cool," I said. We dropped our boards and I let Max lead us down State, as if we weren't really going to follow Beckett. It didn't matter, because by the time we got to the 101 and Michelle's Hill, Beckett Montgomery was gone.

Max looked disappointed, but didn't say anything as we hung a right onto Cabrillo and skated toward the house where the party was.

I decided I'd get him nice and plastered at the party so he could forget about the hippie reggae chick. We had our whole lives to live. Why the hell blow this awesome night for a chick who might be a major head case, or worse? When you're that focused on one person, there's only one way it can end, and that's *badly*.

We skated all the way to Shoreline Park and up Beachfront to the house where the party was. We walked right in without ringing the bell or anything.

The party was going full tilt. There must have been seventy, eighty kids jammed into the living room, bumping their uglies to some stupid music. We moved toward the mob, looking for the beer.

At least, that's what I was looking for. Max was looking all over the place.

"See her?" he asked over the music.

"Dude, just find the beer."

Max scowled but veered off toward a hallway that prolly led to the kitchen. I picked through the crowd and ended up standing in front of this L-shaped black leather couch. A huge flat-screen was mounted on the wall—sweet. But the channels kept flipping, one after the other.

I looked down at the couch, which was entirely empty except for the A-train himself, Anthony Lincoln, who was slouched down and holding up his head with one fist and changing the channels with a remote. He was wearing a Raiders jersey. Max told me once it was his dream to play for them. Well, that wasn't going to happen if next season he played like he did those last few games.

He was on the short end of the L, so I sat on the long end, just close enough for him to hear me.

"Hey man, what's up?"

Anthony's eyes slid over to me and he gave me a backward nod. "Sup."

"Not drinking tonight?"

"Naw, man."

"Cool."

Which wasn't exactly a cool thing to say, but I had nothing else. Man, was this it? Bunch of f'ing dancing to Top 40 and watching TV? F that in the A. I started looking for Max to come back with those beers. No wonder A-train looked bored. This place needed booze, and stat.

Fortunately, some eye candy happened by and sat down next to Anthony. It was that freaky chick Morrigan, who'd just busted up with her boyfriend. That meant she was available. Sweet. Not exactly my type, but cute. Her friend, Ashley, the one Max had shot down last year, was with her.

They didn't even look at me.

"Hey, Antho," Morrigan said as she splooshed down onto the cushion next to him, and Ashley sat beside her. Close enough for me to touch.

Anthony grinned a little and bumped fists with her. "Sup, Macbeth."

I snickered. Good name for her, all gothed out like she was. Big fan of black clothes and eyeliner, anyway. I thought she'd get pissed at him, but she smiled.

"Just getting warmed up," she said, and pulled a pint of Jack from her bag. She twisted the cap off and took a swig, shuddered, then gestured to Anthony with it. "Some?"

A-train shrugged and kept flipping channels.

"You here by yourself?" Ashley asked, leaning over Morrigan's lap.

"Yeah," Anthony said, kind of looking around at everyone like he wasn't sure.

"Where's the team?"

Anthony shrugged. "They'll be by," he said, like he didn't care.

"They still talking shit?" Morrigan asked.

Another shrug. Dude, this guy's shoulders were f'ing huge. "Naw," he said. "They over it."

"That's cool." Morrigan took another sip off the Jack and again tried to hand it to Anthony, who grinned and shoved her hand away.

"Yeah," I chimed in, "they should shut up."

All three of them looked at me.

"Well, they should," I said. "A-train's the boss, right?"

"Uh—okay," Morrigan said, and they all went back to talking to each other. Skank.

"I'm glad you came," Ashley said to Anthony.

"Thanks, sister."

"Yeah, you needed this," Morrigan said. She gestured with the Jack. "And this!"

This time Anthony took it and had a sip of his own. "Goddam," he said. "That's gonna rot your guts out, girl."

"I should be so lucky," Morrigan said.

"Shouldn't you be out and all ravin' or something?" Anthony asked.

Morrigan socked him on the shoulder, which made Anthony laugh. "I'll rave on your ass if you don't gimme my Jack back."

"Tss, naw, you lost it, too bad," Anthony said, all like teasing, and took another sip.

This turned into a wrestling match on the couch, which was kinda funny—this tiny white chick fighting this enormous black dude, like she had a chance in hell. Anthony just kept putting the bottle out of her reach until she got tired and climbed off him. He just laughed at her. So did Ashley.

"I was just *sharing*," Morrigan said. "C'mon, man, I need that to make me pass out."

"There's a keg in the kitchen and bottles outside," Anthony said. "You're too young to be drinkin' this."

"You're like six months older than me!"

"Not my problem." He was grinning.

And Morrigan grinned back at him, like they were best f'ing friends. Man, it's weird who gets along with who sometimes, ain't it?

"I *swear*! I knew I should've just left you here all sulky."

"I'm not sulky."

"You are too. I'm the queen bitch of sulk, man. I know."

"Yeah, whatever."

"We all know that, sweetheart," Ashley said, and flicked Morrigan's ear. I was hopeful for a second they'd start wrestling or something, but they didn't. Damn.

"Hey," Ashley said to Anthony, leaning over Morrigan again. "You okay? We haven't talked a lot lately."

Anthony looked at her. Something went past his eyes, like a thought, you know, but then he just shook his head. "I'm okay," he said. "What?"

"You going to play next year?"

Anthony turned away and flipped the channel one more time. CNN came on.

"I don't know," he said. "Maybe."

"Well, you should," Morrigan said, and stood up. "Serious."

"Yeah?"

"Totally. You're awesome."

This time I saw Anthony wince when she said that. "Yeah, maybe not anymore."

Morrigan frowned at him. "Antho, come on, man. It's been *months* since—"

"Yo, Macbeth, go get yourself some beer, huh? Come on, now. Don't start with me."

"Antho . . ."

"It's a party, girl. Come on, start drinking or something. I don't wanna be talking all serious."

"Then give me back my Jack!"

"Mm . . . naw, I better hold on to it for safekeeping."

"Jerk."

"Yeah, I know."

Morrigan leaned over and gave him a hug, and Anthony hugged her back with an arm the size of a boa constrictor. "All right," she said. "I'll go drink stupid-ass beer then."

Ashley scooted over to A-train and hugged him, too. "You have to have a good time, all right? Not sit here watching TV all night?"

"Yeah, sure, sister."

"Hey," Morrigan said, "you know where that drama department kid is, the one who sells weed? Isn't this his house?"

Anthony gave her a disgusted look. "Don't do that, that's nasty."

Morrigan looked shocked, but recovered quick. "All right, damn! If you say so."

"Hell yeah I say so, *Macbeth*."

She punched him in his rock abs. *"Sulky,"* she said. She turned to Ashley. "Beer outside? Let's make that happen." They started poking through the dancers.

"Hey!" Anthony called. "Come get this Jack!"

"Keep it!" Morrigan called back. "I'll get in enough trouble without it!"

Anthony kinda grinned after them as they headed out to the back patio, then turned back toward the TV. The mute button must've been on, because that closed-captioned thing was scrolling at the top of the screen. Something about the economy. F'ing *boring*.

I moved off the long couch and sat nearer A-train, but keeping plenty of space between us. "Fag seat," I called it. Two dudes can't sit next to each other all close like that.

"So you're playing next season, yeah?"

Anthony cocked an eyebrow and looked at me. "I don't know."

"You should, man, you're real good."

He turned to the TV again. "We'll see."

"I remember that game against Goleta, man," I said. "What was it, like, a forty-yard run? Dude, that was cool, juking all those dudes."

Anthony almost smiled. "Yeah."

"You could take State next year, man, no sweat."

"Maybe."

He took a longer swig from the bottle.

"Too much pressure?" I guessed.

"What's that?"

"Too much pressure," I repeated. "At the games."

"Naw," Anthony said. "It wasn't that."

"Well, what the hell happ—"

"Don't worry about it." He set the remote down beside him

and started rubbing one palm with his other thumb, like his hand had cramped up or something.

The A-train sounded like he was serious, so I shut up. Luckily, Max showed up finally with two cups of beer and handed me one. "About time!" I said.

"It's all crowded in there, man," he said. He nodded to Anthony. "Hey."

Anthony nodded back, then sorta studied Max. "Hey, man, I saw you couple years ago at tryouts, right? Why didn't you play ball?"

"Graduated," Max said.

"Naw, last couple years, man?"

"He was in love," I said.

Max got all pissed. "Shut up!"

But Anthony laughed. "That right?"

"No!" Max said, then stuttered, "I—I mean, yeah, but no, that's not—"

Me and Anthony both laughed at him. I felt bad, but only a little.

"Brother needs to get himself laid," I told Anthony.

Anthony grunted and Max glared.

"He's right, you know," I said to Max. "Maybe you should've played. Got a scholarship or something." I turned back to A-train. "You got any coming?"

"Naw, man."

"How come? You were a great receiver, bro."

"I know."

"Didn't your brother get a scholarship? 'Cause you're way better than—"

Anthony reached out with his left hand and grabbed my shirt in a bunch. I damn near spilled my beer. I thought for sure he was going to deck me right there.

I been in a couple fights here and there, like at the skate park or whatever, but this dude could tie me into a knot, so I just froze and hoped for the best. Anthony didn't even look at me, just held me there by my shirt.

Max moved closer, all business. He was bigger than Anthony, but not half as scary.

But Anthony didn't even look at him as his hand relaxed. He pulled it back. "Sorry, just messin' with you," he said.

"No problem," I said, happy to still have my teeth. *Dude, that was close. I didn't even know what I did!*

I started to get up, but Anthony pointed at the TV with his bottle. "You believe this shit?"

I looked. The news chick was reporting about all these soldiers being deployed overseas.

"Yeah," I said. "That's messed up, I guess."

"Yeah," Anthony said, and took another long slug from the Jack. His eyelids started to droop a little. "Yeah," he said again.

Right about then, this chick Fat Beth started making out with this dude on the arm of the couch next to Anthony. Anthony didn't seem to notice. He just leaned forward and read every letter of the scrolling captions like they were the Raiders' secret playbook.

Damn, man. Watching the *news*. At a *party*.

The Jack was half gone already. So was A-train, for that matter. But he just sat there staring at the TV and drinking.

The scene was getting old. I turned around to tell Max we should hang out on the patio, maybe near those two chicks, who I could see through the picture windows. But Max was standing there like a lighthouse, scanning the crowd, looking for his soul mate Beckett. He had his lame-ass Lucky 13! card out again, wiping it up and down his fingers.

"Dude," I said. "Would you just forget about it?"

"It's gotta be tonight," he said. "I have to do it tonight."

I took a breath to tell him how lame he was when I noticed none other than Beckett f'ing Montgomery creep into the house through the front door. Max's back was to her. She looked like a little animal being chased by wolves or something. She bolted across the room toward a hallway and disappeared. Max didn't see her.

Maybe I should have told him she showed up, but I didn't. What good would it have done? Then he woulda just stood there all night, talking about *this time, this time,* just like he had the last three years, and *hell* if I was gonna listen to that anymore. There was drinkin' to do.

Plus, something occurred to me as I watched Max playing with his stupid card and A-train staring at the big-screen.

"Hey, man," I said as Max toyed with the card and stared hopefully out the windows.

"What?" he said.

"You know thirteen is not a lucky number, right?"

BECKETT MORRIGAN
TOMMY BRENT DANIEL
AZIZE RYAN ANTHONY
JOSH MAX ASHLEY

WE WALKED IN TOGETHER, MATT, JOSH, RYAN, TOMMY, AND ME. We looked badass, like we moved in slow motion to cool theme music. The house was full of people, most of whom I recognized from school. It was really dark, hard to make out faces.

We stuck together and tried to locate the alleged keg that was supposed to be the whole point of the party, but we got hung up in the living room of this enormous two-story house. A ton of kids were dancing and yelling at each other over this gigantic sound system, which was playing, if I'm not mistaken, a really old Social Distortion song. I didn't think anyone else in our school was cool enough to know Social D. besides Josh, even if we did live in Southern California.

Ryan immediately started talking to Bethany Carter, who I recognized from junior English, and within seconds was able to suavely coax a red plastic cup of beer from her hand. Somehow, he made her smile when he did this. What a soldier. A couple of text messages from Super Cuca's and the right smile, and bam. He was hooking up.

Matt and Tommy stuck near to Josh, like they were keeping an eye on him. Josh examined every girl in the room. Looking for Morrigan, I'm sure. Part of me hoped she wasn't here, but another part thought it might be sort of fun. But maybe that cute blond friend of hers had talked her out of showing up. I was in the mood to drink and smoke and chill out with my buds, but I wouldn't mind breaking up what was going to be one hell of a skirmish if Josh talked to his girlfriend again.

Or rather, I reconsidered, his ex-girlfriend.

I looked aimlessly around the room, looking for other people I knew. The only light came from this huge plasma TV, one lamp in the corner, and light spilling in from the kitchen adjoining the living room. It was like being at a miniature concert in here, like a live band was playing. Everyone's faces blurred together, and we hadn't even started drinking yet.

I watched Ryan sit down on the couch with Bethany on his lap. They were all smiles and giggles. They ignored and were being ignored by the guys who also sat there, some skater and Anthony Lincoln, our all-star receiver. The guy had glue for hands, most of the time. He was watching the news, but I could tell the sound was off because those white-on-black closed-captioned letters were scrolling along the top of the screen. The reporter was saying something about how fourteen soldiers—real ones, that is—had been killed that day. Bummer. Anthony was taking hits from a bottle of Jack Daniels and staring at the screen while this skater dude was talking his ass off.

Who comes to a party to watch the news? Weird.

The guys and me started shoving our way through the room toward a sliding door leading out to the backyard. The yard wasn't quite as crowded. Better for kicking back.

"What do you think?" Tommy said as we wormed through the other kids. Matt and Josh followed behind.

"About what?" I said, tapping some dude on the shoulder to squeeze past him.

"See her?" Tommy said.

"Nope, not yet." We broke through the crowd and onto the back patio.

"Guess again," Tommy said, and jerked his head to our right.

Morrigan was in mid-stumble toward Ashley, who was kicking back in a lawn chair. Even at a distance, the blue of Ashley's eyes glittered. She smiled at Morrigan, who collapsed onto her butt and crossed her legs at the ankle, tapping her red Chuck Taylors together in an irritated sort of way. She had a bottle of beer clutched in one hand.

"Might have to check that out in a bit," I said, giving Ashley the once-over.

Tommy grinned and slugged my shoulder, and I slugged him back.

The backyard of this house was humongous by Santa Barbara standards. I didn't know the guy whose house it was, but I knew he was like an actor or something in the drama department. The flyers we'd gotten at school never gave a name, just the address and a Photoshopped pic of the house engulfed in flames under some twisted font that said SHORELINE BEACH PARTY. We were just up the street from the beach and Shoreline Park, but I hadn't seen anyone headed that direction when we pulled up; they were all here, jamming to the music and getting liquored up.

"Hey," Matt said, appearing next to me. "We're gonna maybe hang in the kitchen or something. Thought I saw the keg."

Matt nodded slightly toward the two girls, then gestured back toward Josh with his eyes. Josh hadn't seen them yet; he was still inside the house, behind Matt, and too short to see over anyone and through the large windows that separated the patio from the living room.

"Cool," I said. "We'll be out here."

"What's up?" Josh called from behind Matt.

Matt whipped around and shoved him back into the crowd before Josh could catch a glimpse of Morrigan. "Let's raid the fridge!" Matt said, and pushed Josh toward the kitchen.

Well, it would work for a little while, anyway.

I pointed. "Beer. Now."

"Craptastic," Tommy said.

We walked over to two blue ice chests and helped ourselves to bottles.

Tommy shook his head. "Didn't think there'd be this many people," he said as he popped the cap off his brew and flung it into the bushes. There were maybe twenty other kids standing and sitting in little groups all over the yard and near this awesome brick barbecue on our left. I could smell pot in the air.

"Where should we kick?" Tommy said.

"Wherever," I said, but was trying to find a place where we could watch Morrigan and Ashley. For a couple different reasons.

Tommy gestured to a small hill beside a palm tree, and I followed his lead over to it, swishing over this pristine green grass. We both sat down with exaggerated, old-man sighs, our knees up and dangling our beers between our fingers. For some reason, at that moment, I finally felt like a senior. Like the next year was going to be awesome in a major way, if only Josh would feel better.

And if I could find a cute girl to hang with.

I glanced over toward Morrigan and Ashley. Morrigan was finishing her beer, then opened another while Ashley relaxed and kicked absently at the concrete. Ashley looked stone-cold sober. Morrigan was intent on adding to whatever buzz she already had going, and was talking a mile a minute. I was too far away to make out the conversation, but Ashley kept smiling and nodding her head, as if accepting—as it appeared Matt had—that her job tonight was to keep an eye on her friend.

"I should go talk to her," I said.

"Who?"

"Ashley."

"Go for it, man," Tommy said, and began packing a fresh box of smokes.

"Yeah?"

"Yeah," Tommy said. "Tear it up. Just remember, we'll have our pick of chicks next year, right? Chick picks!"

"I sure as hell hope so, soldier."

"So go talk to her. C'mon."

I shrugged, not wanting to let on how much I wanted to do just that. "Maybe in a bit."

Tommy just laughed at me. He knew I was full of it. Probably my best bet was to find him a girl too, so I'd be free to mess around with someone next year. He hadn't dated since like last summer.

We chilled out and drank and smoked, just like we'd planned. We both drank two more beers and took turns pissing on a tree in the corner of the yard. I was careful to make sure Ashley didn't notice me doing that. She and Morrigan were still hanging out on the patio, and Morrigan had kept her drinking pace even with me and Tommy. She was definitely swaying by the time I was finishing my third, and had gotten up to stagger around the patio while she continued her speech to Ashley. Ashley was cool, never leaving her chair or drinking a drop.

"Hey, man. You hungry?" Tommy slurred after a while.

"I could eat." It had been some time since we'd stopped at Super Cuca's. And the beer was already working on me.

"Let's order a pizza or something," Tommy said.

"Sounds like a plan."

Tommy pulled out his cell and called information for the closest pizza place, and had them connect him. He ordered a couple of something called Monster Meat pizzas for delivery.

Right then, out of nowhere, I heard someone scream *"Fuck you!"* at the top of her lungs.

Everyone, including me and Tommy, looked. Then I laughed. Morrigan was screaming at her hand. I imagined her hand taking on a life of its own like in that *Evil Dead* movie. It hit me she was holding a cell phone, screaming at someone on the other end of the line.

Ashley got out of her chair and held out her hand as if to take the phone, but Morrigan wasn't having any of it. She moved away from Ashley, stomping into the yard, coming closer to me and Tommy, but clearly not having any idea we were there.

"You din even notice!" she screamed as she got nearer to us, kicking up bits of grass. She had a bottle of beer in her other hand, and was swaying quite a bit. Morrigan's a pretty small girl, so those beers she'd chugged had her a little drunk.

"I fugging sneaked outta my rum like hours ago and you din even fugging notice!"

So, okay, probably a lot drunk. Her words were slurring together all over hell. My first semi-drunk thought was, Why would she be fighting with Josh over the phone when he was in the kitchen? Tommy and I reared back and watched

Morrigan's performance, but everyone else in the yard had dismissed her.

Ashley walked quickly over to Morrigan and tried to wrestle the phone away from her, pleading, but it wasn't working. Morrigan was one drunk chick on a tear, and no one was going to ruin her moment of glory.

I was kind of impressed. Whoever was on the other end of the line was really taking a beating.

"Every day it's like that an' . . . an' . . . stupid! Stupid sports an' stupid Barbies! You know sumthin'? Ashley was right! You never even hugged me! *Asshole! I hate you!*"

It hit me through the alcohol haze I was in that this wasn't Josh she was talking to.

It was her dad.

Ashley managed to pry the phone away from her. Morrigan pulled back her arm and let the beer bottle fly against the brick wall. It shattered and sent a couple of stoners scattering for cover.

Ashley held the phone up to one ear and plugged the other with one finger. Her face was serious, tilted down, trying to put a verbal bandage on what was sure to be a monumental ass-whipping when Morrigan got home. I felt like, frankly, she deserved one, but not necessarily for being at this party. For how she treated Josh, yeah.

Tommy and I sat there, watching the drama. Wish I could've heard the other side of *that* conversation. I wondered if her screaming would catch Josh's ear, but figured the music inside was probably too loud.

"No, she's fine, we're just at this party," I heard Ashley say as she walked by me toward the patio again. Morrigan was already on her way there, holding her head in both hands. I got the impression she was crying, or about to, but when she turned around, her face was red with drunken rage. She was talking out loud to no one.

I could barely make out what Ashley was saying as she walked away. "Yes, I knew she snuck out, but . . . no, she's fine. No, I'll bring her home. I will. No, you don't have to come get her. No. I swear."

She walked out of range. I kept watching her. Ashley looked to be putting up a hell of a fight for Morrigan, who by this time had settled down into the lawn chair. Morrigan might be a bitch, but she had a hell of a friend going to bat for her.

I had nothing better to do until the pizza got here, and figured one of us should be near the front door to get it anyway, so I got up and wandered toward Ashley to listen in. She was near the coolers, so I went for a beer and pretended to fumble with the cap. At least, I think I was pretending. I had a pretty good buzz going.

"We've been gone since like eight o'clock, don't you think that's a little odd?" Ashley said into the phone.

There was a pause.

"No, it *is* my business, because you never pay any attention to her. She was practically crying about it over dinner."

Pause.

"I know she's your kid, why don't you act like it?"

Pause. Head shake.

out toward us from the house, a worried look on his face. Matt came crashing after him.

Josh went straight to Ashley.

"What is it, what's happening?" he said, all breathless.

"Josh, it's nothing," Ashley said.

"It's not nothing, what's going on? Morrigan's in the kitchen screaming like a witch. Who's she talking to?"

"Her dad, okay?"

Josh squinted at her. "What's the problem?"

Ashley sighed. "Morry snuck out of the house to come here tonight, and now her dad wants to come pick her up."

"She really snuck out?" Josh asked, looking confused. "She's never done that before. Never had to."

"I think that's part of the problem," Ashley said.

I started giggling a little as this other chick showed up behind Matt, who was blocking the doorway. I could see her trying to get past him without touching him or saying anything. I sort of recognized her from school. Or at least, I recognized her clothes. She had this weirdo striped hat on. All I really knew about her was that she didn't talk much.

"Yo, Matt," I said. "Make a hole, soldier."

Matt looked behind him and stepped out of the way. The freaky silent chick squeezed past and wandered out onto the patio, looking around at everyone. She stopped cold when her eyes hit Ashley.

Ashley stared right back at her. Me, Matt, and Josh looked from one to the other. A new drama? Should've sold tickets to this bash.

"Hey," Ashley said.

"Hey," the silent chick said. I could barely hear her.

"What're you doing here?"

"Ashley . . . ," Josh started, but Ashley held up a hand.

"Shut up for a second, Josh, okay?" She took a few steps toward the other chick. "So what's up? I didn't think you'd . . . it's been a while."

"Ashley!" Josh shouted. "Listen!"

"God, what?" Ashley shouted back.

"I know Morry's dad, okay? He's got to be the boss. If you don't let him come get her, it's just going to be worse, okay? So would you please call him and tell him where she is?"

"I'm sorry, I should . . . ," Silent Chick said.

"Beckett, wait, hold on," Ashley said, and looked at Josh. "Josh, I've known him a lot longer than you have, okay? Are you *sure* you want him coming here?"

"Well, I mean, I'd take her home, but . . . well."

Ashley lifted her hands and shook them, like she needed some space. "Okay, okay, fine. I'll call him in a few minutes, okay? Where is Morrigan?"

"Still in the kitchen, I think," Matt said. "Talkin' to some skater."

"I should probably just go," Josh said. "I don't think we should meet up."

"I thought you saw her in the kitchen," I said, and stifled one hell of a beer burp.

"She didn't even see me," Josh said, trying to look like this fact didn't bother him. "I could clear out now before she does. You guys want to go?"

"We got a pizza coming," I said.

Josh looked disappointed. But hell, we were already here. We could get a ride later. Maybe from Ashley.

"Better check with Ryan, too," Matt said, which to me sounded like he was saying, *Because if Ryan's staying here and you're taking off, that means I can start drinking.*

"Yeah, okay," Josh said. He looked from me, to Matt, and back to me. "Well . . . see ya," he said, and pushed back into the house.

Ashley watched him go, then turned back to the silent chick. Beckett.

"Sorry about all that," Ashley said. "Morrigan's having a bit of a meltdown."

"I should really go," Beckett said. I could barely hear her.

"You could hang out," Ashley said quickly. "We could talk."

"No, no, I should just go home." Beckett turned to go back inside.

Finally! I thought. But just as I was gearing up to keep talking to Ashley—probably a bad idea under the circumstances—who should come back out to the patio, completely skull-bombed?

"Hey!" Morrigan said as Beckett stopped. "Iss my bess friend! My bess friend's bess friend. Wass up, *chica?*"

"Oh, god—Morrigan . . . ," Ashley said, and moved to intercept her.

Chicks, man. I went back to the coolers for a fresh beer—

I'd finished the last one—and Matt joined me. We could still see the whole show.

Morrigan slapped a hand down on Beckett's shoulder. "You doan have my cell number, do ya? Get yer phone out, *chica*. Put my number down. An' gimme yers. So we can *hang*."

I felt bad for poor Silent Chick. Sincerely. She looked scared half to death, so scared she did exactly what Morrigan said and typed her number into Morrigan's cell. Who knows if it was the right one.

"Cool!" Morrigan shouted as she took the cell back. "Now less sit right back and hear a tale about why you fuggin' ditched my girl?"

Ashley sighed while Whore-igan looked all drunk and sassy at the quiet kid. Ashley took a step toward Beckett.

"Look, can we talk later tonight? After I get Morrigan settled down?"

"I—I don't know," Beckett muttered. "I need to—"

"Beck, come on."

"I'm sorry, I really need to go, okay? I'm sorry." She turned and started trying to work her way into the house.

Ashley stared at her back, her eyes wide and unblinking.

"So we're going to do this again next year?" she shouted suddenly. "You ignoring me?"

Interesting! The drama continues. Should've brought a camera.

Beckett stopped, her shoulders bunching up around her ears. "What's the go?" she whispered. Whatever that meant.

I don't think Ashley heard her, but Morrigan did. Morrigan's head snapped up, and seriously, fucking *bayonets* shot from her eyes.

"Just another year of pretending like I don't exist?" Ashley went on, folding her arms and not seeing Morrigan's death glare. I could see just a little of Ashley's tan skin through the gap in her overalls. Sweet.

"Because that's just great," Ashley said. "It's great to know that all those years didn't mean *anything* to you. Thanks."

Ouch. Chicks, man.

Guys got it so easy. Things go wrong, we yell, then punch each other on the arm and that's it. Chicks, not so much.

Beckett turned back around, but looked at the concrete, the trees in the yard, the stoners hanging by the barbecue, anything other than Ashley.

"I—I just . . . it's . . ."

"Say words!" Ashley shouted.

Morrigan belched, covered her mouth, and giggled. "I'muh dainty lil flower," she announced, and narrowed her eyes at Beckett. "How 'bout you, flower girl?"

"Morrigan, shut up," Ashley said.

Beckett shook her head wildly. "I'm sorry," she repeated. "I can't be here."

"So take off then," Morrigan blathered. "Thass whatcher good at." She slung an arm over Ashley's shoulder. Taking possession.

But Ashley shrugged it off and stomped away, sitting down in the lawn chair and holding her head in both hands.

Me-*ow*, right?

Beckett finally looked up, and locked eyes with Morrigan, whose own eyes were half shut but smoldering.

"Well?" Morrigan said. "Git goin', *chica*. You could go smoke some ganja, mon!" She cackled, then tripped over her feet and fell square on her ass.

Good, I thought with a grin. Too bad Josh missed it.

And then Beckett, without hesitating, reached down and hoisted Morrigan back up to her feet. Morrigan stared at her, and yanked her arm away.

"Excuse me, *what's the go?*" she said, whatever the hell that meant. She stumbled back a step and added, *"Bitch."*

Beckett flinched, and shot a disbelieving look to Ashley. Ashley just grabbed handfuls of her hair and squeezed her eyes tight. "Morry . . . ," she said, and shook her head.

"Nice hat, *mon,*" Morrigan said to Beckett, and started laughing. Off balance again, she crashed into Matt, who shoved her back the other way. Morrigan just kept laughing. Man, talk about *hammered.*

Ashley reached out for Beckett, who backed off toward the sliding door again. "Sorry," Beckett whispered.

"Man, hell with this," Matt said under his breath, and headed for Tommy. I followed him, looking back at the girls over my shoulder.

We went back to the little hill where Tommy had been watching the whole ordeal and laughing his head off, so I had no idea if the quiet kid, Beckett, said anything else. It would've been cool if she'd started a catfight, though. Wouldn't mind breaking *that* up. After a minute

"Hey!" I heard Morrigan shout as we walked over to Tommy. "Anyone know where Ryan Bru-Brunner is? He's fuggin' *hot.*"

"You're shitting me!" Tommy said, and went on laughing.

Matt, on the other hand, whirled around, the cords of his neck popping out. "He's upstairs!" Matt shouted back at Morrigan. "Go fucking find him, bitch!"

Whoa. Never seen Matt like that. He sat down and spat to one side.

"What's up?" I asked as I watched Morrigan flip us off, toss her phone to Ashley, and dive back into the party. It looked like Ashley was apologizing to Beckett, who took one step back for every step forward taken by Ashley.

"Just sick of it," Matt said, really pissed. "I know she's drunk and whatever, but Jesus, I mean . . ."

"Yeah, you're right," I said.

Beckett kept backing away from Ashley and eventually turned and went inside. Ashley, alone, rubbed the back of her neck and went over to where she and Morrigan had been hanging out. She shoved Morrigan's phone into a black satchel thing on the ground. Then she opened her own cell and dialed. A second later she stood up and went into the house.

"Man," I said. "Those cats are messed *up.*"

"Told ya," Matt said, and drank about half his beer.

Tommy sat up, wiping his face, as his laughter finally died. "What a night," he said. "What a *party.*"

"You're hammered," I informed him, and belched.

That set Tommy off again, and I joined him. A second or two later, Matt started in, too.

"So where's Joshua?" Tommy asked, blinking rapidly through his laughing tears.

"Taking off," I said.

"Craptas . . . tastic," Tommy said. "That sucks. We're supposed t'be watchin' him."

"Aw, you miss him? Wanna walk him to his car?" I said, and took a nice long drink.

Matt laughed at that, so to retaliate, Tommy shoved me, making me slosh some beer. "Duce!" I said.

Tommy looked all pissy for a sec, but then started laughing again and clinked his bottle with mine. See what I mean? Chicks go all mental. Guys, we drink together and leave it at that.

We had a semi-coherent conversation about where to go this summer to get out of town for a while, but mostly we burped and played Dead Leg. At one point, I saw Ryan come out onto the patio and grab Morrigan's black satchel thing and go back inside, but none of us called out to him. Actually, we dove behind the little hill to hide, like a prank, which was really dumb since Ryan clearly wasn't looking for us.

Probably because of all the beer we drank, I completely forgot about the pizza until the cops showed up.

AZIZE

BECKETT MORRIGAN
TOMMY BRENT DANIEL
RYAN ANTHONY
JOSH MAX ASHLEY

IT IS NINE O'CLOCK WHEN I PULL UP TO THE HOUSE. It's a nice neighborhood, nicer than mine. The houses east of State Street are better, more expensive. That is why I live on the west side of State. My mother and father and I all work to support the family, and have only a two-bedroom condominium. One day, I will buy one of the houses east of State Street. Or perhaps a palace on the beach or in the mountains, with enough room for my entire family, even those who must live in Türkiye.

But we're fortunate to live here. I know this. And although the dark blue Civic in the driveway of this house is polished and gleams under the streetlights, the light blue Bug is not in as good condition. So these are not rich people. That's good news. *Zengin* do not tip very well.

I run up the redbrick path to the front door and ring the bell. No one answers, so I ring again. It takes many moments for a tall white woman to answer. I can hear a television turned up loud somewhere nearby in the house.

"Hello," I say to her, and smile.

She smiles back, folding a newspaper page under her arm and placing a yellow pencil in her hair. "Hi."

I pull one pizza box from its red insulated bag. "Fourteen eighty-six," I tell her. I make sure to continue to smile. This is Ata's advice, and he is right. Customers appreciate it when you smile.

"Okay," the woman says, and begins to dig through a large feminine wallet sitting on top of a side table.

Then she frowns. I've seen this frown before, but I continue smiling.

"Oh dear," she says, and turns away from me, shouting into the house. "Honey, do you have a twenty?"

Something important happens on the television, because the person she is shouting to cheers *"All right, go, go go!"* very, very loud.

"Jim!" the woman shouts.

"What!"

"I said, do you have twenty dollars for the pizza?"

"What? No!" the man shouts back.

"Oh, that damn ball game, can't hear a thing," she says. She turns to me and smiles, embarrassed. "I'm sorry, would you wait just a quick minute for me?"

"Of course, ma'am." My cheeks are beginning to hurt, but I won't stop smiling. If I'm fortunate, she will find her *yirmi* and give me the entire bill for making me wait.

"Oh, great, thank you . . . ," she says, and peers at my name tag. I don't like my name tag, mostly because it's attached to my white shirt, which is tucked into my white pants. This uniform makes me crazy, but it's part of the job, so I don't complain. Ata says I was lucky to find a job, and he's probably right.

"Ah-zee-zee?" the woman asks.

"Ah-zeez," I correct her politely.

"Oh, I'm sorry . . ."

"It's no problem!" My cheeks are burning now.

The woman sets her wallet down on the table inside the door, and I put the pizza box on top of the red bag because it's beginning to burn my hands. The woman walks down a hallway, calling.

"Morrigan!" she shouts. "I need that money I gave you this afternoon."

Morrigan? I know that girl. She is very . . . spirited, Ata would say.

The woman turns a corner, but I can hear her knock on a door. "Morrigan?" she calls again. "Morry, I need that twenty. We ordered pizza. Morrigan?"

I am running late now. I need to get back to the pizzeria for the last part of my shift, which is attending to the counter, filling orders for carryout. Kabara—my boss—will not be happy if I'm late. Neither would Ata if he knew. My father wants me to be sure to bring honor to our family by working hard, and even though it's been almost five years since we left Türkiye, I still want to make him proud of me.

"Morrigan!"

The woman is gone for several minutes. I hear doors opening and closing down the hall. Suddenly she comes around the corner and rushes into a room just beyond the front door, the room where the television is on. The hardwood floor squeaks loudly beneath her bare feet.

"She's gone!" the woman yells.

I hear the man's voice. "What?"

"Morrigan is gone, Jim. She's not in her—would you turn the TV down for just one minute?—she's not in her room, she's not in the bathroom, she's *gone!*"

"Oh, for hell's sake," I hear the man say, and then he appears, barefooted and wearing plaid shorts and a T-shirt. He does not look at me at all as he goes down the hall calling Morrigan's name. The game has gone to a commercial for large, manly pickup trucks: *Made in America,* a deep country-western voice says, *because it matters.*

I didn't know when I drove here that this was where Morrigan Lewis lived. There must be one thousand people named Lewis in Santa Barbara, how should I know that this was her house?

I don't care too much. Morrigan has never spoken to me at school, so I am not exactly upset she is not here.

Mr. Jim Lewis is gone for several more minutes. The woman, Mrs. Lewis, comes back to the door looking very, very angry.

"Um . . . I'm sorry, we're having a bit of, um . . . trouble here, do you take credit cards?"

"Of course, ma'am!" Even though I smile for her, she doesn't seem to notice. I get the strong feeling my tip will not be very large.

I trade her card for the pizza box, which she takes and dashes away with, probably to the kitchen. By the time she comes back, I've already run the card through my portable machine and have a receipt and pen waiting for her.

Mr. Lewis comes back from the hallway. "Well, where is she?" he demands from Mrs. Lewis.

"Well, I don't *know*, Jim, obviously!"

"Why is the screen off her window?"

"What?"

"I said why is the screen off her window, were you cleaning in there?"

I am ready to get in my car and go, but I need Mrs. Lewis to sign the receipt. I wave the pen. "Ma'am?"

"What? Oh." She takes the pen and receipt, scribbles her signature, then hands the pen back to me. "No, I wasn't cleaning in there, you think she'd let me into her room?"

"So she snuck *out*?" Mr. Lewis shouts.

"Ma'am?" I ask politely, because I need the receipt she has just signed.

"Oh, god, she probably went off with Ashley," Mrs. Lewis

says. "She went to that party." She then swears, using the name of God again.

"What party?" Mr. Lewis says.

"Jim, I swear, do you not hear a word she says to you?"

"*Me?*"

"Ma'am," I say again, a little louder. I'm now many minutes late for the last part of my shift.

"Look, it's simple, call Ashley," Mr. Lewis says.

That must be Ashley Dixon. I know her, too. But like Morrigan, I've never really spoken to her. I believe she is an acquaintance with Beckett, a girl I know from school who shares her comic books with me. Beckett has mentioned her before, but only in passing.

"No . . . no, I'll just call Morrigan, find out where she is," Mrs. Lewis says, and starts to close the door. She has not looked at me once since going in search of the twenty.

I put my hand on the door to stop her. "Ma'am, I apologize, but I need to take your receipt, please."

Mrs. Lewis stops and turns to me as if I've magically appeared on her doorstep. Then she shakes her head and stretches out her hand.

"Oh, I'm sorry, here," she says, then closes the door without saying goodbye.

I hear both of Morrigan's parents shouting instructions at each other even as I turn to run back to my car.

"Here, give me the phone."

"Jim, what if she doesn't answer? How will we find her?"

"Oh, she'll answer. You *bet* she'll answer!"

I wonder if I've done the right thing. I know exactly where Morrigan is, if she has indeed gone to tonight's graduation party. I have the directions in the pocket of my shorts at work, in my locker. Should I have told Mrs. Lewis that? I hesitate at the door, listening.

"Morrigan! Where the hell are you?" I hear Mr. Jim Lewis shout.

"Jim, please calm down," Mrs. Lewis says, and then they must walk away because I can't hear them any longer.

I head back down the redbrick path. It's none of my business, and I do not need to be known as a *gammaz*, a tattletale, when school begins again in September. Some reputations are bad no matter what country you live in, and being a *gammaz* is one of them. I have trouble enough making friends. But in September I'll be a senior. Perhaps it will be easier then.

I get to the pizzeria and check the receipt. No tip.

Annoyed, I relieve a coworker at the counter who is looking quite bored. It's a slow night for a Saturday. He is happy to leave the counter to me and smoke a cigarette beside the garbage bags in the alley.

The door opens and I pull on a big smile, ready to greet the customer. I'm surprised at who it is.

"Hey," Beckett Montgomery says as she approaches the counter.

I'm embarrassed to be seen in my uniform, working, but I try to hide it. "Hi, Beckett," I say. "How are you?"

"Oh . . . okay. I didn't know you worked here." She sets her woven purse on the counter.

There are no other customers. And my boss and two coworkers are in the back. I have time to talk.

"Yes," I say. "Did you want something to eat?"

"I thought I'd grab a slice of pizza. You sell pizza here?"

I laugh. "I think so," I say, and she smiles just a little bit. That makes me proud.

"Oh!" I say. "You know your friend Morrigan?"

Beckett blinks. "Morrigan Lewis? She's not my friend exactly . . . why?"

"I just delivered to her house. I think she sneaked—or snucked?—out of her room to go to the party tonight."

"Really."

"Her parents are . . . pissed off."

"Wow."

"But—she is not your friend?"

"Well . . . not . . . really. She's friends with a—an old friend."

"Ashley."

Beckett looks surprised. "You know her?"

"No. You have mentioned her before. In the library."

"Oh. I didn't realize." Beckett looks at the floor for a moment, then up at me. "So, hey, are you going? To the party?"

I laugh again. "Who isn't!"

"Me."

"No? How come?"

Beckett shrugs. She is a pretty girl—a very pretty girl—but there is no romance between us. That's okay. Ata will not allow me to date a girl who isn't Muslim anyway. That's a problem in Santa Barbara. When I go to school in Los Angeles after graduation next year, where there are more people like me, I hope it will be better.

"I don't know anyone," Beckett says. Her voice is soft. A whisper.

"You know me!"

"Yeah, but you're cool and junk."

"You think I am cool in this uniform?"

"No."

We both laugh again. It is not loud, but feels nice.

"But you read cool comics," Beckett says.

"As do you," I remind her.

That is how we met, back in November. We were both in the school library reading comic books. I was reading *Incredible Hulk*, and she was reading *Batman*. We often have fun arguments about which superheroes would win in an imaginary fight, especially those from different publishers. Bane versus Wolverine, for example.

"The new Batman movie looks good, doesn't it?" she says.

"It does. I am looking forward to it."

"I wish they would've done the Hush series, though. That was awesome."

"I remember. You made me read it in one sitting! I was late to math class."

"But it ruled, didn't it?"

"It was very good. Perhaps they will still make a movie out of it."

"I love the Superman fight," Beckett says.

Now there is a sentence not many girls in the world would

ever say, and certainly none where I am from. You see why I like Beckett Montgomery? Even though I have no desire to take Beckett on a date, I am still jealous of and happy for the man who will. I am quite sure she has no boyfriend, though. She has never talked about boys. Or family.

"I don't think Batman can defeat the Hulk," I tell her.

"I don't know . . . he's pretty smart."

"The Hulk can lift tons and tons of weight! Batman cannot even punch him."

"Says you," Beckett says, and begins to smile again.

"How can you like Batman so much?" I ask her, to tease. "He is just a spoiled rich white man!"

Beckett stops smiling. I feel terrible. I have said something wrong, but not because English is my second language. It's the content of what I said that's hurt her.

"I guess I just know where he's coming from," she says, looking at the floor again.

"You don't look like a spoiled rich white man, my friend."

"It's not that."

I'm not sure what this means, but I don't like that she is hurt. I decide to change the subject.

"Well, I think you should go to this party." I try to sound firm the way my father does when he is telling me something "for my own good."

"Yeah?"

"Yes!"

"I don't know," Beckett says. "I feel like . . ."

She hesitates. I wait for her to continue.

Beckett shakes her head. "Like it doesn't matter. I had my chances to meet people and I didn't, so why bother?"

I do know what she means. I've felt that way before. Indeed, if I did not have Beckett to talk to about comics, I would hardly talk to anyone outside my family or customers.

But I didn't know she felt this way, too.

"What about your friends?" I ask. "Ashley?"

"Um . . . yeah, well, the thing is, I haven't talked to Ashley in a really long time."

I didn't know this, either. "Oh," I say. "But you mentioned her. Several months ago. You said you wish you could call Ashley. You do not talk to her often?"

Beckett shakes her head. "No."

"Did something happen?"

Beckett looks at me sharply. "What?"

"I mean, between you and Ashley."

She relaxes, and I am glad. I don't want to make her angry. I don't think I would like her when she was angry. Much like the Hulk.

"Oh . . . no. No, not really. We sort of grew up together? And then . . . some . . . stuff happened, and I didn't talk to her for a while . . . I was really busy . . . then Morrigan moved here and they started hanging out? So we just sort of lost touch, I guess."

It is clear to me there is much more to the story, but I hear my boss coming this way from the kitchen.

"That is too bad," I say, and grab a pencil. I gesture with my eyes so Beckett will understand that I do not mean to cut her off. She's a smart girl. She nods quickly and looks up at the menu.

"Okay, so . . . one slice of cheese pizza," she says.

"One slice cheese," I repeat, and ring up her order. "Two thirty-six."

She pulls a small coin purse out of her bag and sorts through change. She assembles two quarters, four dimes, and several nickels and pennies.

"Oh," she says quietly. "I don't think . . ."

My boss walks past me. "See ya tomorrow, Azize! Good work tonight!" he calls, and heads out the front door.

I say goodbye to him, and wait until I can no longer see him on the sidewalk. Then I reach for the coins and push them back toward Beckett.

"It's okay," I tell her. "Tonight is on me." I feel cool when I say this, like a TV star.

"No, no. No, I can't," Beckett says, and wipes the change back into her bag, skipping the coin purse. "Thanks, but it's okay."

"Beckett, no, it's no problem."

"No, it's cool, I should have brought more money," Beckett says, and begins to leave.

"Beckett!" I say. "Wait!"

She pauses by the door with one hand on the handle.

"What about the party?"

"I don't know," she says.

"Please. Come. I will be there. You can talk to *me*!"

"Maybe," Beckett says. "Bye."

She leaves quickly, walking along the sidewalk, her head down.

I'm certain I've done something wrong, but I cannot decide what.

The rest of my shift is uneventful except for two skateboarders. The smaller of them wants to know if I'm permitted to drink alcohol. I am not, and I don't mind. But I don't tell him so. The entire time, I am thinking of excellent American *küfür* words to call him, but I am on the clock, and there are two of them, so I take their order and let them leave again without saying any of my excellent words.

So many people do not understand my country. Many do not even know where it is. My family is "Middle Eastern," that is all they say, which is not really accurate. And because we are "Middle Eastern," my father, Ata, is looked at with suspicion when he purchases propane for our patio barbecue. I once yelled at a man *much* larger than me for asking my father what he was going to do with the propane. I was so angry! I felt like the X-Man Colossus, wrapped in living steel, wanting to tear this ignorant man apart with my bare hands. But my father pulled me outside and shook my shoulders and told me to control my temper, to not yell at people like that, even if they were ignorant.

I asked him why. He said to me, "They are afraid and angry, Azize. And when people are afraid and angry, they do stupid things. We must forgive them. Do you understand?"

I did, but I also did not. So I nodded my head and promised him I would not yell at people again when they treated him like a criminal.

These two skateboarders . . . they were not suspicious of

me. They didn't look afraid or angry. But the smaller one, he was making fun of me, I'm sure of that.

And they are going to the party tonight. I'm not sure I wish to go if they will be there.

I hate many things. Rap music, which makes me wince. Also ricotta cheese, diet soda, war movies, people who don't tip, and the state of Arizona. But of all things I hate, I hate ignorance most of all.

I'm minutes away from finishing my shift when our telephone rings. I answer it, and take down a delivery order for two large Monster Meat pizzas. When I hear the address, I almost laugh. It's the same as the address on the flyer in the pocket of my shorts in my locker.

I put in the order, and stare at the address. Should I go to the party? I wonder if Beckett has decided to go. If I knew that she would be there, perhaps I would go. I don't have a phone number for her, so I cannot ask.

I make up my mind. I'll go to this party, and I will make one new friend. That will make Ata proud. Maybe I will convince Beckett to do the same. That way when we begin school again, we won't be so alone anymore.

I go to the back room and change my clothes, telling my coworkers that I will deliver the pizza myself since I'm going to that address. They are surprised, but grateful. This means they will not have to make another trip. Since the order was made with a credit card, the register will cash out correctly. When my coworker asks about the tip, I laugh and tell him he can have the whole thing if he wants. He accepts this. He knows I am a man of my word.

State Street is still filled with people as I leave work and drive toward the house where the party is, near Shoreline Beach. The drive is quick. Beyond my windshield, down Beachfront Avenue, past the intersection with Shoreline Drive, I see the Pacific, cool and black. Lights from the oil platforms and a yacht shine through the darkness like earthbound stars.

I will have a boat like that one day. *Dr.* Azize Hasan al-Fanari. I'll buy my father a new home so he can retire, and my mother her own fabric store, and myself a boat. I will pay to have all my relatives move here to where it is safe.

I don't miss Türkiye very much, and I do not miss Arizona at all. Not one iota, however small *that* is. I never imagined living near a beach. A beach with sand, real sand, not the Sonoran Desert dust that makes up most of Phoenix. No, the beach is home now. I confess I hated my father briefly for moving us here. But it took only one trip to the beach right before I started high school three years ago to change my mind.

You were right, Ata.

That's what I said to my father when I returned from my first visit to the beach. My father had smiled and hugged me tightly. I wouldn't say it to anyone, but I like when he does that. I like making him proud. "You have done the right thing," he says to me sometimes, like when I joined Academic Decathlon or earned this job. It is my favorite thing he says to me. It means I have honor.

• • •

I slow down as I near the house where the party is. Both sides of the street are lined with cars. Some are "parental-rentals," others are cheap first-timers with band stickers stuck along their rears. My own cheap white hatchback, which has no stickers, is one such first-timer, purchased by my father so I could find work more easily. Work and school are priorities as far as my father is concerned. I don't mind; I'm smart and I like having the extra money. I don't get an allowance.

I stop the car and pull the emergency brake, parking behind a red Blazer. I can hear music even before I open my door. The house is thumping with it.

I jog up the front walk, balancing the large red insulated bag in one hand, and approach the front door of the enormous house. Drunken shouts assault me through the walls. Bass music shakes the very ground. It is no trick to imagine the beautiful girls dancing inside.

You need a good girlfriend! my mother likes to say. *When will you get a good girlfriend, Azize?*

Perhaps never, I think as I carefully push the door open. With my father's insistence on dating only Muslim girls, my options in Santa Barbara are not many. I know my mother knows this, and secretly I think if I dated another girl, a girl who was not Muslim, my mother wouldn't mind. Ata is another matter.

Maybe instead of NHS and Academic Decathlon, I should have gone out for football. The girls seem to like that. And who wants to date a brain, anyway? A pizza delivery brain, at that.

A brainiac Turk pizza boy.

God bless America!

I walk into the foyer and set the pizza down on a side table. There is no way to know who ordered the pizza, but it will be eaten, I'm sure. I look at the people gathered—so many! It is so dark and so loud. It is almost exactly how I have imagined a party to be. I've never been to one like this before, but there were flyers for it all over school, as if the entire school was invited. It looks like most of them have shown up to dance and drink.

Ata knows I am here. I didn't even try to lie about it. Why should I? Ata trusts me.

I look for Beckett, but no person is distinct from another. I see only acne faces and hormone eyes. All alike in the dark. All except for one person, leaning against a wall near the front door and nodding his head in time to the music. I recognize him as the larger of the two skateboarders who had come in for pizza earlier this evening. He wasn't a bad guy.

I remember my pledge to make a friend, and I walk right up to him. "Hello," I say.

He looks at me and his face shows surprise. "Oh. Hey, man."

"Look," I say, holding up empty hands, "no alcohol."

He is confused for a moment, but then grins. "Hey, dude, I'm sorry about that. Brent can be a dick sometimes, he don't mean nothin'."

"It's no problem," I say, and offer a hand. "My name is Azize."

"Max," he says, and we shake hands. I am surprised at how

easy it is to introduce ourselves. Why have I not done it before? Suddenly, I feel next year might be very good for me.

I look around at all the people again. "Max," I say, "do you know Beckett Montgomery by any chance?"

Max glares at me like I have insulted his mother. "Do *you?*"

Suddenly, I feel next year might not be very good for me after all. Why do I never know why I make people upset?

"She is a friend. We talk in the library at school sometimes."

"Is she here?" Max says, very agitated. He looks all around.

"I don't know," I say. "That's why I asked."

Max sneers, but not at me, exactly. "Oh, right. Naw. I ain't seen her. So, you're just friends?"

"Yes."

"You're not like goin' out or nothin'?"

I laugh. "No! Just friends."

Max nods, and looks relieved. "Cool," he says. "Sorry if I snapped at you."

"It's no problem. So you have not seen her either, then. Hmm."

He shakes his head. "Been in the kitchen, mostly." His eyes seem to lose their focus for a moment. "I don't think she's comin'."

He looks very unhappy.

"She could be in that crowd," I say, and point to the students who are dancing wildly in the living room. "We would never know it."

"Yeah . . . that's true."

"I will look around just in case. Should I tell her you are looking for her if I find her here?"

Max looks panicked. He licks his lips and stutters for a moment.

"Well—yeah. I mean, I guess. Sure. Well, wait. Naw. I mean, I guess. I dunno."

I see now.

Max has a crush on my friend. I can understand this. There have been many girls at school I wish I could talk to, but I never have. Perhaps tonight will be different.

I decide to help Max. It's a good way to become friends.

"If I find her," I tell him, "I will try to make sure we come this way. Then you can talk to her if you wish."

Max nods slowly. "Yeah. Okay. Sure. Thanks."

"It's no problem," I say. "Have fun."

He nods again, and I move further into the crowd of people. It is impossible to tell if she is in the group dancing in the living room. I push myself through the crowd to the patio door and look out to the backyard, but do not see her there, either.

Disappointed, I decide I might as well check the rest of the house. This is just the type of house I would like to buy someday. Spacious, clean, wealthy. I wonder what it looks like, upstairs and down. How it is decorated. I will look for Beckett and take mental notes for my palace.

I move through the crowd again, this time headed for the hallway and staircase that lead out of the living room. I glance around for Max, but he is not where I left him. I walk down the hall: bathroom, occupied. An empty bedroom. The hall turns left, and I follow it. Another bedroom, another bathroom. This house is endless! I am jealous of whoever lives here.

I see a dim light shining from behind a half-open door.

I listen closely, in case there are two people inside *getting together*. But I hear nothing, so I go for a closer look.

It is a beautiful office, with a dark wood desk, a plush black leather chair, and two leather seats. Two of the walls are filled with books, law books mostly. And curled up in one of the two leather seats is Beckett, with a copy of *Batman* in her hands.

She looks up, startled. "Oh!" she says, and adds, "Azize."

"What are you doing hiding back here?" I ask with a smile, and sit across from her.

She winces. "I don't know," she says. "I don't know what I'm doing here at all, to tell you the truth."

"I don't believe parties are meant to be spent alone reading comics. I believe that is for school hours."

She quite nearly grins, but still looks unhappy.

"What book is that?" I ask.

"Oh, it's old," she says. "*Year One.* Just rereading it. What's it look like out there?"

"Crowded. Very crowded." I think of Max, somewhere out there hoping to talk to her. "You should come out. Say hello to people."

"I think I'm just going to go home in a little bit. I should never have come here."

"Beckett," I say, "please forgive me, but I must ask—what is it you are so upset about?"

"I'm not upset."

"You are not happy."

She shrugs, then sighs. "Can I tell you something?"

"Of course. You can trust me."

"I have to drop out of school."

"What? For what reason?" Education is terribly important in my family. My father would destroy me like the Hulk if I said I would drop out of school.

"I have to go to work," she says.

This, I understand. Work is only slightly less important than school to my father. And that is only for now. Education exists to prepare us for work, so one day, work will indeed become most important.

"I see."

"I only came tonight to kind of say goodbye, I guess," Beckett says. "Except it turns out I don't really have anyone to say goodbye to."

"Is there no other way? To finish school, I mean. You must have a diploma."

"Maybe online sometime down the road. I don't know."

"Well, if you do drop out, I will miss you next year."

"Really?"

"Of course!"

Beckett gives me a small smile, and I am proud. "Thanks," she says. "That means a lot to me."

"But before you go," I say, and stand up, "I really do think you should try talking to some more people out there. Introduce yourself to someone new. I did. It was rot so bad."

"Yeah?" she says. "Well, I'll think about it. Listen, don't tell anyone I'm back here, okay? I don't want to deal with it."

"I won't," I say. "But I give you only five minutes. Then you must come out and say hello to someone."

"*Ten* minutes."

I smile. "Very well. Ten minutes."

"And I get to go outside. It's way too loud and all smoky inside."

"Okay," I say. "Ten minutes, then we go to the backyard."

"Thanks."

I smile again, and leave her alone. She is such a nice girl. But it is also clear she would rather be alone.

I go back out to the living room and look for Max. Should I tell him to go to the office? That would seem the nice thing to do. But if he wishes to be romantic with her, now is perhaps not the best mood to catch her in.

I am still thinking this when someone bumps into me from behind. Hard. I almost fall over.

I turn around. The person behind me is African American, and approximately the size of Bane, the villain who broke Batman's back. He wears a silver and black jersey of the Oakland Raiders.

This person says nothing, only stands there glaring down at me. After a moment, he leans toward me, and I recognize him as one of the popular football players from school. I do not know his first name, but I think his last name is Lincoln, because I've seen it on his jersey as he runs for touchdown after touchdown at our home games.

"Hey," Bane/Lincoln yells in my face. His breath stinks of liquor. "You brung that pissa?"

"Yes," I say.

"We got pissa fromma terroris'. Anybody order pissa from a terroris'?"

I stand still. My mind aimlessly flips channels of response. No one else seems to hear us, but I see the other skateboarder, Brent, who came into my store. He is sitting on the couch, watching us, his mouth hanging open as if he is in shock.

That is probably the same look on my face right now. Rage churns my stomach.

"*What* did you call me?"

Lincoln tosses a palm into my shoulder. The blow, while not a punch, pushes me toward the front door. It does not hurt, not exactly, but it feels like a sledgehammer.

"Best take that outside," the football player warns. He looks me up and down. "Towelhead terrorist motherfucker."

I begin to shake. My arms and legs grow cold. A silent home movie unspools in my mind. My father, bloodied, on the floor of his own store back in Phoenix, weeping inconsolably. This was many years ago. Back then, and even now, I do not know whether he weeps from the beating he has received from two local ignorant cowboy-type men or from the fear and anger at their ignorance. They used the same words this football player has.

I have never talked to my father about that day. But the

movie springs into my thoughts and will not go away, like a DVD that keeps skipping on its track.

We had moved to California the following month. *It will be safer in Santa Barbara,* my father said through bruised and swollen lips. *People there are not like they are here, Azize. You'll see. Too many cowboys in Arizona.*

The cold in my limbs is melted by sudden fire, and I scream. I willingly forget my father's teaching to forgive. This ignorant football player cannot get away with these words! My mouth chooses the words of its own accord. I have no control, I am enraged.

"You are a fucking nigger! You goddam ass! Who are you? Fuck you, nig—!"

Lincoln reaches for me, but someone else slides in between us.

It is Max.

"Whoa, whoa, whoa," he says, and puts a hand on Lincoln's chest. "Chill out, bro."

Lincoln snarls. My body quakes with adrenaline.

"Look," Max says to me, "maybe you better take off, dude. Okay?"

"Did you hear what he said?" I demand. "Did you hear what he called me?"

"Bro, this is a really *big* dude who just polished off a bottle of Jack all by himself," Max says to me. "Let it go. Just call it a night, okay?"

Lincoln is still staring at me. I feel we are two fighters being photographed for an upcoming match. Max's words sink in, though. This football player is enormous. I am not afraid of him, but he is clearly the stronger of us. He looks as though he would like to tear me limb from limb.

"Okay," I say. "I will go. But he is wrong! He is the asshole!"

"Sure, he's wrong, no sweat," Max says. "Just call it a night."

I glare once more at Lincoln, thinking of some more excellent *küfür* words, but instead turn and go to the front door. I go outside, slamming the door hard behind me.

I mutter to myself as I go to my car. Where is the justice? I have done nothing! What does this American football player know of terrorism? Nothing! He should spend some time in Türkiye, perhaps in the southeastern provinces with my family, before he calls me such a name. I am an American, too! I want to tell him. Not that he will listen. He is like the cowboys in Arizona.

I do not like Santa Barbara as much as I did when I woke up this morning.

I open my car door and climb inside. I realize through my rage that I have forgotten about Beckett. I am supposed to go bring her out to the party in a few minutes, escort her to the back patio to meet someone new.

I cannot. If I go back inside, there will only be trouble. I hear my father's words in my head. *We must forgive them, Azize.*

Before I am able to close my door, a hand pulls me from the car and throws me to the street. My keys clatter away. My chin scrapes against the blacktop.

"What you got now, bitch?"

Lincoln. He has followed me outside.

Good! I will defend myself.

I jump to my feet, but Lincoln is on me in a heartbeat of time, a brick fist smashing my face, my ribs. The pain is immediate, intense, but far away. He holds an empty liquor bottle in his other hand. He needs only one to defeat me. Adrenaline protects me from feeling the worst of it, but I know I am hurt. I hear parts of me crack inside.

I fall to the road on my hands and knees, stunned and gasping for air. My sternum feels like breakfast cereal. Bells jangle in my head.

Get up. I must get up.

Get. Up.

His foot crashes into my thigh, taking the limb from beneath me and sending me face-first into the street. I taste oil. Blood. Another kick lands on my hip, another on my shoulder. All three areas sting momentarily, then ache and knot under my skin.

Get up! Fight him!

I swing a meaningless, impotent fist at his feet, which are now in front of me, but Lincoln is out of reach.

"You juss stay right there," I hear him say. And I watch as his sneakers walk unsteadily toward the front door.

No! I will fight back. He is drunk. I can fight him! Ata does not understand that these people speak only one language. That sometimes there is only one way to make your point and stand up for yourself!

I push myself up and lunge for Lincoln. I swing as hard as I can at the back of his head. My knuckles crack against his skull. I wait for him to fall to the ground, unconscious and defeated.

Things do not go as planned.

Lincoln whips around, touches his head where I hit him, and says, "Sum'bitch."

I turn and try to run for my life. I have no choice. It is clear now I cannot defeat him after all. His drunkenness has made him impervious to attack, not uncoordinated and weak as I had expected.

Maybe this is why Ata tells me to forgive. Because I would live longer.

I don't even think of heading for my car, I just run as fast as I can down Beachfront Avenue toward Shoreline. But I am trying to outrun a person who runs for a living. Delivering pizza and reading *Hulk* does not build up the same muscles as playing football.

Lincoln *is* the Hulk. I am the smarter but weaker Bruce Banner.

I hear him stampeding behind me. Terror gives me speed, but not enough. We pass all the cars parked on the street for the party as I run blindly toward Shoreline Drive. If I can make it there, I will be safe. Surely. I can run to the park across the street, put something between us, try to talk to him. Apologize for what I have said, even if he will not. That is what a smart man would do.

I do not get the chance.

His body crashes into me from behind, taking us both to the ground, where I inhale the taste of grass of a stranger's lawn. My breath is expelled from my lungs. I hear more than feel something snap in my rib cage.

I am smothered by the full weight of my assailant. I hear glass shatter over my head, splitting my scalp. He pummels my skull, opening a gash on my forehead and smashing one ear to pulp. I feel each blow ricochet down my spine, dull thumps that spin my eyeballs in their sockets.

I'm sorry, Ata. I'm sorry.

At last there is a pause, long enough for me to realize with some detachment that my consciousness is fading. I lie motionless on the grass, feeling blood pour down my face and neck in a gory bath. Shards of glass glitter in the grass.

I hear him speak through ragged breaths. He has spent himself on destroying me.

"Think you bad, huh? Yeah. Not so bad now, are you, mother? Shoulda keep your ass shut, huh?"

He kicks me again, and the pain in my ribs explodes, as if those shards of glass are rammed into my lungs.

He throws me onto my back and wraps one hand around my throat. I pry at his fingers, but it is useless.

Is this what my father felt?

I am sorry, Ata.

Tell my mother that I—

"Thass what you get," I hear him say above me.

I see a light appear. Beautiful light. It outlines the football player from behind, giving his body a dim halo. It is perhaps a superhero, using a superpower to destroy him.

It is light, light like on the boat I will buy when—

BECKETT MORRIGAN
TOMMY BRENT DANIEL
AZIZE **RYAN** ANTHONY
JOSH MAX ASHLEY

By the time I was able to start making out with Bethany Clark ... wait, Carter ... in an upstairs bedroom, I was under the influence of about five beers. We started on the couch, but this big dude Anthony Lincoln was taking up most of it, staring at CNN and clenching his hands. The news! At a party! Weird, man. It took three beers for me and two for Bethany before I convinced her to check out the bedrooms in this place. The couch was too small for all three of us.

The truth is, there are three things to do at a party: drink or get high, fight, and get laid. Or variations on them. And the other truth is, we only drink or get high so that the next day, no matter what asshole thing we did at the party, we can say, "Oh, I was drunk. Sorry." And people buy it. It's the stupidest excuse in the world. You still chose to drink. You knew going into it you wouldn't be yourself. That's why you do it.

But there's this little sober part of you that you can still hear, this little voice that is thinking totally clear and going all like, *You can get away with grabbing that chick's ass. You can get away with coldcocking that assclown from French class. You can do it with this chick because the next time you see her, you can claim Drunk.*

Which is exactly what I'm going to do the next time I see Bethany. After she is done getting me off.

Bethany's what they call a slag in England. Good word. It fits her. I'd had an eye on her for a few weeks, and I picked her right away as someone who'd put out. A few too many extra pounds, not a lot of girlfriends, you know. Looking for anyone to pay attention. Hey, it beats the hell out of what happened to Josh. I lost track of him as soon as we got here, but even at Matt's house, he was all bent out of shape.

No thanks. No way I'm letting a chick do that to me. No way.

And I'm nice to them. The girls. I don't treat them bad. I may not stick around, but I don't ignore them after, either.

This is taking too long, and starting to hurt, mostly because I'm drunk. Also because Bethany isn't exactly a supermodel.

So why bother?

Because why not. I still get what I want, so what the chick looks like is hardly relevant.

Don't go getting all judgmental on me. If Josh acted more like me, he wouldn't feel like he does right now. He'd feel—

Ohthankgodherewego.

There. Finally. Cripes, I barely even felt it, I'm so hammered.

Ah, well.

"Wow," I say to Bethany, to make her feel good.

"Yeah?" she asks. She smiles.

"Sure," I say, and give her a quick kiss on the forehead. "That was awesome."

She giggles. I feel bad then, so it's time to go. But Bethany beats me to the punch.

"I needa beer or something, you want something?"

I shrug and nod. Why not. I give her what I think is a smile, but I can't feel most of my muscles.

Bethany gets dressed and I just lay back and close my eyes. Maybe I'll just pass out right here. I won't be the only one passing out tonight, I'm sure.

"Be right back!" Bethany whispers.

"Cool," I say, and relax. This is awesome. I could use a smoke, but they're in my jeans and that would mean getting up. Too wiped out to bother. I'll have Bethany grab them for me when she comes back.

I'm not sure how long I was lying there, because time does funky things in the postcoital, post-hammered seventeen-year-old mind.

The door, which Bethany didn't close all the way, flies open, and wakes me right up.

"The hell!" I shout. I am buck naked, and light from the hall falls right across my junk.

The chick who careens into the bedroom is not Bethany. Too skinny. Her shirt is pulled up—she's holding the edge of it over her head with one arm, right in the middle of taking it off. Her face is covered by the shirt. Narrow midriff, neon white skin, smallish tits in a shiny black bra . . .

The chick giggles drunkenly and smashes into a closet door.

"Oop, fuck," she blurts, and then finally is able to pull the shirt over her head and toss it to the floor.

Oh, sweet holy shit.

Morrigan?

She slams the door shut and stumbles to the bed as I scramble for sheets, the comforter, a pillow, anything to cover up with.

"Now this's more like it," she slurs, and throws herself on the bed. She carries a bottle of beer, which sloshes some out of the opening. The other hand is reaching for me.

"Whoa!" I shout, and scoot to the other side of the bed. I manage to flip on a bedside lamp. "Morrigan, what the hell are you doing?" And *shit* do I want my clothes back on, like, *yesterday.*

"Lookin' for Ryan," Morrigan says, and even though I've put down a few tonight, her beer breath is *rancid.* Her free hand reaches under the pillow I'm holding against my crotch. "Foun' you! Yay!"

I grab her arm. "You're drunk."

"Uh . . . yeah! Kiss me."

I try to look into her eyes, which are swimming behind half-closed lids. "Do you know who I am?"

"Ry-own! Like, right on! C'mon, kiss me."

She leans toward me.

This is, um—*bad.*

. . . Because she is still pretty damn cute.

So, okay, there's that moment. I feel it every time. That moment you know you should stop what you're doing, but your prick always wins. You can't help it.

I'm still holding her arm down on the mattress, but she's leaning toward me trying like hell to pucker her lips.

I think about it.

I do. I admit it. She's cute, sue me. And even though I'm a little achy from the marathon with Bethany, I still feel that little jump down there, like when your body's saying, *Oh yeah, here we go!* even if your mind is saying, *Dude, don't do this.*

Josh's ex-girlfriend.

I know I can't do this, even though I want to. She gets closer, closer.

I take a deep breath, ready to get up and put my damn pants back on, when someone knocks on the door and it opens again, just a crack.

Oh, great. Try explaining this little scenario to Bethany. This'll take some—

"Hey, man . . . you still in here with Bethany?"

Ah, *shit.*

"Josh," I say.

"Bethany in there?" he says.

I stare at Morrigan, who's still pawing at me.

"... Noooo," I say, because that's not a lie even if it's not the entire truth.

"Cool." He opens the door all the way and walks in. "Listen, I'm gonna take off—"

Then Josh freezes solid when he sees us. The moment is a photo, a 3-D picture absent of sound or motion.

"Jesus," Josh says. Which is odd because even though Josh swears better than anyone I know, he never "takes the Lord's name in vain" or whatever you call it. But looking at me on the bed here, I can't say that I blame him.

His face goes blank, and it creeps me out. He moves, and he moves fast.

It's not that I'm afraid of him; dude's like two foot three. But *he's* wearing all his clothes and ten-hole Docs. I'm wearing a *pillow.*

"Dude" is all I have time for.

Josh sprints over to me and lands one solid right in the sweet spot under my left eye, which sends me to the carpet, cock a-flyin'. I haven't even shaken my head before he's around the other side of the bed next to Morrigan.

"What'd he do to you?" I hear him say. My eyes are pretty much rolled back into my skull and apt to stay that way until after college.

Morrigan pauses, and I pull myself to my knees, hidden behind the bed and holding my face. *Damn,* that hurt. Kid's got some guns there, who knew?

Morrigan looks over at me, like she can't believe what Josh just did. Hell, *I* can't. Well—okay, I can, but still.

Then she gets that trademark Morrigan smart-ass look on her face, turns to him, and says, "Everything you wouldn't."

Ah, shitballs, you *dumb*—

"Dude!" I say again, holding up my other hand to ward off another attack.

But Josh just backs away, with that same non-expression on his face.

" 'Kay," he says. "So be it."

He looks over at me. Glares. Works his jaw behind closed lips.

For some reason, I can't say anything.

"You," Josh says finally, then hesitates, snorts a bit, and laughs. "Fuckin' prick."

Then he turns out of the room and is gone. I can hear his feet crashing down the staircase, full speed.

"Shit," I say, and scramble to find my clothes.

Morrigan falls back on the mattress and laughs. "Ah, c'mon!" she says. "Less juss do it, Ry! C'mon, it'll be fun."

"Shut! Up!" I yell, and finally manage to pull my jeans on just as Bethany walks in.

Good god.

She takes a look at half-naked Morrigan on the bed, me zipping up, and tosses two cups of beer on my chest. Then she smacks me right where Josh decked me.

"Ass!" she screams, and barrels out the door, hysterical.

"Oh, come *on*," I whine, and use the pillow to wipe beer off my chest.

"We're alone, we can do it now," Morrigan says, sliding across the bed toward me, then tumbling to the floor, ass over elbows, giggling stupidly.

I ignore her, yank my shirt over my head, and run out the door.

Morrigan screams, like she's been shot or something. *"Why not!"* she shrieks behind me. "WHY WON'T ANYONE—"

Whatever. I roar down the steps at top speed and crash into someone. She screams, and something flies out of her hand and lands in the middle of the throng of kids dancing. Even over the music, I can hear the crunch of plastic beneath their feet.

It's Ashley Dixon. She whirls toward the dancing group and covers her forehead. "Ohhhh, that *sucks!*"

"Sorry," I say, and run to the front door. I throw it open and head barefoot down the redbrick path to the street, looking for Josh's Blazer.

Gone. I hear tires screeching down the block.

I squat down, lacing my fingers behind my neck like I'm going to be arrested.

This is, um—*real* bad.

"Hey!" Ashley calls. A second later she's standing beside me. "What's the go? You broke my phone!"

"Sorry," I say again. "I didn't mean to smash you like that."

"Well . . . it's okay. Sorta. What're you doing?"

I stand back up. "Looking for Josh."

Ashley blinks, then looks suspicious. "He took off," she says. "Came running down the stairs and bolted out the door. He's gone?"

"Yeah. 'Fraid so."

"What happened?"

"You wouldn't even believe me."

"I might. What?"

"Frankly, Morrigan just tried to bed me."

"Oh, god. Are you serious? Wait—and you *didn't?*"

"No, I didn't!"

"You do have a bit of a reputation. . . ."

"Yes, maybe I do, but I didn't touch her. Josh busted in and it probably looked . . . bad."

Ashley shakes her head, and actually laughs a little. "Well, isn't that perfect. I can't believe this night. Where's Morrigan?"

"Probably passed out in a bedroom upstairs."

"Any idea where Josh might've gone?"

"None whatsoever. He was . . . I don't think *shocked* is a strong enough word. Son of a *bitch*."

"You or Josh?"

"Oh, cute."

"Sorry. Look, can I borrow your phone? Mine's trashed. I was in the middle of giving directions to Morry's parents."

I turn back toward the house and we walk together to the front door. "Directions? Why?"

"Long story. They're bent. She snuck out of her room to be here tonight."

"So take her home."

"Yeah, tried that. They were too pissed. They want to kill her themselves."

We get back indoors and tromp up the stairs. I let Ashley go first so I can keep an eye on her ass. Sue me. "So they're on their way?"

"Sort of. I told them we were at a house near Shoreline Park, but that's when *you* cut us off."

"Well, I'd think seriously about getting your little friend to sober up some. She's *gone*."

We get to the second floor, and I put a hand out on the wall to steady myself. Ashley smirks at me. "You're not so steady yourself, Romeo."

"You're a lot cuter when your mouth is closed."

"Really? Well, I'll just file that under Go Screw Yourself."

I laugh. I can't help it. Ashley grins, and we go back into the bedroom. Morrigan is, in fact, passed out cold on the mattress. She's tangled in the red tank top she took off a few minutes ago. Her beer has spilled onto the mattress between her legs, creating an unflattering illusion.

Ashley moves toward her and peers at the stain. "Uh—is that beer?"

"I think so," I say, and pick up the empty bottle. It was almost full when she came sloshing in here.

Ashley picks her up under the shoulders and moves her to a sitting position. Morrigan grunts, her head lolling on her neck.

"Hey," Ashley says. "Morry. Wake up, sister. We got to get you home."

Morrigan makes a sound like, *"Harrugh?"*

I search the floor for my cell, which had fallen out when

Bethany and me were undressing each other. It's under the bed. I pull it out and flip it open.

"Who're you calling?" Ashley asks as Morrigan slowly comes back to life.

"Josh."

"Oh. Good idea."

But all I get is his voicemail. I shut my phone and hand it to Ashley. "No answer," I say, and reach down for my socks.

"Aaaaash?" Morrigan wheezes.

"Yeah, girlfriend. I'm here."

"I don't feel very—"

Now, I've had my share of nights worshipping the porcelain deity after a night of boozing it up with the guys. But never have I seen puke that color, or projected with such force. It's the stuff of torture porn. And the noises . . . man, I will remember this night until the day I die if for no other reason than I will never forget the sound of that poor chick puking her guts out onto some stranger's bed at the biggest party thrown this year in Santa Barbara.

Serves her right.

"Well, shit," Ashley says hopelessly.

Happily, I was too far away to get any splashback. "Not much of a drinker, is she?" I inquire nicely.

Morrigan interrupts with three rapid inhalations—and pukes again. Most of it ends up on the floor beside the bed. A line of beer-puke-drool literally connects her lip to the carpet.

Ashley rolls her eyes at me and tosses my phone back. She

manages to get Morrigan to her feet and into the adjoining bathroom, where she sits her down on the toilet lid and starts searching for towels.

I finish getting my shoes and socks back on. "Anything I can do?" I call to Ashley. "*Other* than help you clean that up?" The room's starting to stink something fierce.

She's wringing a towel out in the sink. "Actually, yeah," she calls back. "Could you find Morry's bag? It's that black messenger bag thing. She left it on the back patio."

"I'm on it," I say, and head back downstairs.

The party is going strong. It takes me almost a minute to walk twenty steps through the crowd to get to the patio. Morrigan's bag is sitting next to a lawn chair—amazing someone didn't take it. I grab it and head back upstairs.

"Here," I say, and drop the bag at the foot of the bed.

Ashley has Morrigan mostly conscious now, and looking green. "Thanks. Could you check to make sure her phone is in there?"

I poke around in the bag. Going through a chick's stuff is a bad idea, no matter what. They keep gross stuff in there. But I find the phone without much trouble and hold it up for Ashley to see.

"Thanks," she says again.

"Yeah," I say back. "Listen, I'm gonna—"

"Could you bring me her bag?"

I pick it up and bring it to her in the bathroom. Ashley opens it and dumps the whole thing on the floor, and starts sorting through clothes and stuff. All business now, she pulls off Morrigan's tank top—still damp with beer puke—and tosses it in the tub. I knew Morrigan wasn't a . . . well, *big* girl, but she fills out her black bra pretty nice, I have to say.

Ashley catches me and gives my shin a kick. "Out," she orders.

"Right, sorry," I say, and walk out of the bathroom, closing the door most of the way. But then I stop and lean back against the bedroom wall beside the doorway. "It's sorta weird, isn't it?"

"What," Ashley says from the bathroom as Morrigan moans sickly.

"Josh and her," I say. "I mean, she wanted to sleep with him and he turned it down? That's not natural."

"He has his reasons," she says, and I hear a zipper and Ashley struggling to get Morrigan changed into the cutoffs and black T-shirt that were in her bag. I want to look, just to get an idea of what Josh was passing up, but I don't. I'm in enough trouble as it is, and I didn't even *do* anything.

"I know," I say, "but it's still weird, you know?"

"Are you coming to a point any time in the near future, or are you just waiting to cop another peek?"

I grin. I like how Ashley can be honest without being a bitch. "No point," I admit. "I just think that most girls would've been impressed, not pissed."

"Yeah, well," Ashley says, and opens the bathroom door. I turn. Morrigan is half asleep on the toilet, changed into her spare clothes. "*I* was impressed. I think she was too, in a way. I don't think she knows *what* she wants."

"She broke his heart, you know."

"Yeah, I know. Ick, I need to wash my hands."

She goes back into the bathroom to clean up.

"She should reconsider," I say. " 'Cause Josh is a good guy."

Ashley doesn't say anything. Maybe she can't hear me over the faucet.

"Hey, why does Josh hang out with you guys anyway?" she calls.

"What the hell does that mean?"

"I mean I thought he hated drinking and smoking and all that."

"I never heard him say that. He just doesn't want to. He never tried to make us stop."

The water stops running. "I guess that makes sense," Ashley says. "I never heard Morry complain that he tried to make her stop, either."

"Yeah, well, he's cool like that, and she should have known it." I start heading for the door. "I'm gonna get out of here."

"Sure," Ashley calls back. "Thanks, Ryan."

This stops me cold. *Thanks?* "Uh ... for what, exactly?"

Ashley comes out of the bathroom and shrugs. "I don't know. For not being a jerk."

"Oh," I say, a bit surprised. "Yeah, sure."

"You could've taken advantage of her, you know."

"Yeah ... maybe."

"No, not maybe. Look at her. Hell, *I* could take advantage of her right now."

"Say! That would be hot."

Ashley manages a tired laugh. "You're such a boy," she says. "Okay, sicko. If you're going to be nasty, at least give me a hand with her."

I can't help grinning as Ashley and I pick Morrigan up and walk her out of the bedroom. I feel bad for whoever's party this is, because they've got a hell of a mess to clean up in that bedroom.

Halfway down the stairs, I realize the music has stopped. It is freaky quiet in the living room. On instinct, I slow down as we continue down the steps. Anthony Lincoln, who'd taken up most of the couch earlier when me and Bethany were on it, is blocking the hallway with his huge girth. Over his shoulder, I see a cop walking this direction.

I fight the urge to breathe into my palm and smell my breath. Dead giveaway, that. So I just stop and wait to see what happens next.

Pretty sure the party's over.

BECKETT MORRIGAN
TOMMY BRENT DANIEL
AZIZE RYAN **ANTHONY**
JOSH MAX ASHLEY

I'MUNNA KILL THIS TOWELHEAD BITCH.

It only takes one hand to choke him, squeezin' hard like when I lift. He try to stop me but he too small. His eyes are closed, but I want 'em to open, to see me doing it.

I get all lit up. Headlights.

I juke to the right and fall in some bushes to hide. This big ole red truck speed past. Too fast to see me or this kid lying near the curb.

The kid moves. Pulls his head up. Rubs his throat, tryin' to breathe. It sounds gross. Wheezin'. He roll over and just lay there all breathing hard and coughing.

I almost killed him.

Tss. Whatever. He's done. Just gotta wait till those two kids go back inside. What they doing out here anyway? That dude look mad, hunkered down like that. That girl—shit, that's Ashley. I can't let her see me out here like this. She might tell my—

They stand there talking. Finally they go back inside. I get up and run back to the house.

My knuckles are busted up good. I head for the bathroom. I open the door and the bathroom smell like ass.

I wash my hands. Knuckles hurt. Head hurts.

I touch my head in the back. Comes back bloody. Like my knuckles.

My fingers cramp. Won't be catching a ball any time soon. They might be busted.

You better go check on that boy.

I know who that is. Shut up. You ain't really here.

You tellin' me to shut up, little man?

I squeeze my eyes shut tight. Feel like the drunk is draining out of me.

I can still hand you your ass.

The hell you buggin' me for?

'Cause you mighta killed that boy.

So what, Mike? He had it coming.

You started that shit, son.

"They started it," I say out loud. "Don't tell me who started somethin', bro. They started that shit and that's why you're—"

That ain't why, bro.

I gotta get my bro out my head. I open my eyes and keep washing my hands. They hurt bad.

You remember last time we all talked on the phone?

Before I came home?

"Yeah," I say.

What did I say to you?

My head aches. Like I got tackled. Except I did the tackle this time.

Go on, Antho. What did I say to you?

I remember. Mike couldn't call much, so it was cool when he did. We talked about the Raiders. Fuckin' RAID-AHS! Shit season as always. But we talked about them anyway. I'd play for them one day, I told him. You should've too, I told him after he joined up.

"No can do, brother," Mike said. "Got business to do."

Never made no damn sense. Why did he have to join the Army? "Why, bro?" I asked him when he was packing his bag last year.

"Somebody got to, Antho."

"Yeah, but why you, bro? We're in a good place here."

"Somebody got to, little man. Got to set this shit straight, you know? A whole lotta guys died so we could be in a good place, know what I'm sayin'?"

I didn't like the sound of that. While he was packing, I asked him when he was coming back.

"It's only four years," he said.

"That's a long time," I told him. "What about football?"

"It's all right," he said. "You'll be okay. You take care of Mama. You the big man in the house now."

I tried. Tried real hard. Played ball hard. Kept my grades

up and everything. 'Cause Mike told me to. 'Cause Private First Class Michael A. Lincoln told me to.

What did I say on the phone that last time, Antho?

I remember. I told him to kill some towelheads for me. And Mike got all up in my face about it.

"Don't ever say that, Antho!" he yelled at me. "Don't you ever go say that."

"How come?"

" 'Cause you say that shit and what I'm doin' over here don't mean jack. You know what I'm sayin'?"

I didn't. He was there to kill bad guys. That's what I thought. Except that isn't what he said that day on the phone.

But I just said, "Yeah, okay," and then we hung up.

That was the last time I talked to my bro before he came home. I was having a perfect season till then. Because of me we started losing.

It wasn't right. I couldn't be out there playing when Mike was home again after just a year. Couldn't run and catch when Mike was home in a wheelchair, home learning how to do things left-handed.

If I was there right now, I'd serve you your ass one-handed.

"But you're not," I say out loud, looking at my face in the mirror. "You can't even walk, bro. *You got no fuckin' legs.*"

That boy might be worse off. Then what you gonna do?

"He ain't dead," I say. If I'd finished choking him out like I was planning, then yeah.

You don't know that.

"You hear what he said? You hear what he call me?"

I heard what you called him, dummy.

I got nothing to say to that. He's right. My older bro, he's right all the time. Right about everything except being in the Army. Fuck your Purple fuckin' Heart, Mike. I don't want it.

I know what you want, bro.

"What's that?" I say.

You wanna go back. To before I got fucked up.

What you did out there ain't how to do it.

"How do I do it then?" I wish I was still drunk.

By bein' a man, bro. Be a man.

I was a man. I kicked that bitch's ass.

That ain't what I mean and you know it.

"You're a soldier," I say. "You're a warrior, bro. The hell you want me to do?"

I ain't callin' people names. You know better.

"They almost killed you," I say. My face feels all hot. Damn, I don't wanna be all cryin' in here.

That boy didn't.

"Shut up, Mike."

He shuts up, wherever he's at. But he says one more thing.

Make it right, little bro.

I flush the john just to have some noise. Get Mike out my head. I rub a bunch of water all over my face.

It's been a few months now and I still can hardly look at him. I hate how Mama looks, like parts of her body were torn off, too. I love my mama, and I don't care who knows it. She did good. Raised us up right. Moved us outta L.A., made us go out for teams. Mike was a QB back in the day, working on a scholarship to UCLA. Then he went and joined the Army. Kicked ass there too, just like he did on the field. Went to Ranger school. My bro was a badass. Right up till he got damn near killed.

Mama never should've let him go. But no one was stopping Mike once he made up his mind. All it got him was blown up.

Army said he prob'ly saved a bunch of his buddies. Gave him a Purple Heart and everything. Like that matters now. He was an athlete before he was a soldier, and he'll never catch a ball again, not for real, not with only one good hand. He'll never run again. Never play pro ball.

But that was my brother. Always trying to do the right thing.

Always trying. Already he was calling people around town, YMCAs and kids' clubs and stuff, looking for a way to help kids who can't walk learn how to play games or whatever.

I never hear him complain. He still thinks he did the right thing by joining up.

Aw, shit.

What the hell did I do?

It's that skater dude's fault! I was just watching TV, minding my own damn business. Dude sits next to me and he's all like, "You were a great receiver, bro. Should get a scholarship. Didn't your brother get one?"

Yeah. Mike was supposed to go to UCLA. He might still go, but it won't be on any football scholarship.

We were watching TV and it was like I couldn't even hear the music playing in the room. Didn't care about the dancing going on. Just wanted to get drunk. To forget.

The news came on, and it talked about how these soldiers got killed. That just reminded me of my bro. How close he came.

"You know what?" I said to this skater dude.

"What?" he said.

"I wish I could kill some fuckin' towelheads," I said.

"Yeah, man," he said. "They're weird 'n' shit. Can't even drink beer."

"Oh yeah?" I said.

And he nodded and said, "Yeah, I asked this dude tonight and he was all like, 'No way.' "

"What dude?" I said.

"This pizza dude workin' on State," he say. "Maybe he's coming here tonight."

"I'd kick his ass," I said.

But I didn't mean it. I never kicked anyone's ass *off* the field. Big black mother in Santa fuckin' Barbara, yeah, right. That would be bad. Plus I got football. Take out my aggression. Till Mike came home. Then I couldn't catch a cold, let alone a pass.

The skater just laughed and slapped my shoulder like we were friends. We're not. But I don't do anything, I just watched the news and kept drinking Morrigan's Jack that she gave me earlier.

But then that guy did show up. And the skater was all like, "Hey, man, that's him. I don't believe he showed up 'n' shit."

I looked over at this Arab guy and it's like I can see him killing Mike. Killing my bro. Setting up a bomb on the side of the road.

I got up and went over to him and the skater tried to stop me. He was all like, "Dude, whatcha doin', don't start nothin', he goes to our school, he cool," but it's like I couldn't stop myself. I went over there and bumped into him and hoped he'd start a fight 'cause I wanted to beat his ass for what he did to Mike.

"Well, there you go," I say to Mike as I sit on the john lid. "You seen that? All I did was bump his ass and he went off on me."

You didn't have to get up, little man.

"You would've got up," I say.

No I wouldn't. You know that.

He's right. He wouldn't've.

"God damn, Mike," I say. My head hurts like hell.

Do the right thing, bro.

"Naw way, man."

Then you live with it. And you tell Mama.

Then you come tell me. To my face.

"C'mon, Mike."

I know, bro. I know. I got your back.

But you're gonna have to tell me sometime.

I take out my phone and call emergency. Tell them this guy got his ass kicked, he's probably lying in the street or someone's yard. They ask me all kindsa questions, and I tell them the truth. My name, where I'm at, everything.

Then I hang up and sit there like a pussy. Alone in the bathroom with blood on my hands.

You done good, bro.

"Yeah, I hope so," I say to Mike.

I sure hope so. Because now I'm in this. Big-time.

I sit there on the john while people bang on the door wanting to come in. I just sit there, let them knock. There's other bathrooms, this house is huge.

After a while, I step out of the bathroom and head down the hall. I don't even know where I'm going.

"Antho?" someone says.

I turn around and it's Ashley again. My friend. Her bro and my bro played ball together. You remember that, Mike? You and James, *Jay-maz*, tearing up the field? Ashley's carrying Morrigan, helping her walk with this other guy's help. I should've made her take the Jack back. I should have.

"Hey," I say.

"What's—are you okay, you look . . . What is it?" Ash says.

I lift my hands. Knuckles all skinned. Fists shaking. I can't stop them.

"I fucked up," I say. "Aw, Ash, I fucked up bad."

Ash looks over at this dude, and he takes Morrigan in his arms. She looks almost passed out. I wish I felt that way. But I'm awake. I'm wide awake and sober and I'm scared. I sweated out the Jack beatin' on that kid, but my stomach feels bad now, all twisted.

Ash takes my wrists in her hands. Her fingers don't even go all the way around. Why am I so fuckin' *big*?

"Anthony, look at me. What happened? Why are you bleeding, who hurt you?"

Hurt me?

Hurt *me?*

I can't help it. I fall into her, almost knock her over, push her to the wall, grabbing her in my arms. Need to hang onto something. Someone.

"I didn't mean to," I say into her hair. "I swear, girl. I didn't mean to." Goddam pussy. Some Ranger I'd be. Some fuckin' Raider.

"Didn't mean to what?" she says into my chest. "Antho, what happened?"

The music shuts off all the sudden. It gets real quiet. I look over Ashley's shoulder.

Two cops are standing in the doorway looking out at everyone. All them kids.

Then they look at me.

Aw, shit, Mike.

I could take these cops out. They can't stop me. Nobody stops me on the field, they can't stop me now. I could push right past them and be gone, man. Just be gone.

Make it right, little bro.

"Mike, man," I say out loud.

I got your back. You just make it right.

"Mike?" Ashley asks me, and she looks scared. "What about him?" She looks at me, then the cops, then me again. She looks so worried. Like she thinks I gone crazy, talkin' about Mike like that. She's got such pretty blue eyes. She and James and their parents, and Morrigan . . . they're the only ones I told about Mike. Far as anyone else knows, he's still out there fighting. Wanted to tell the team, tell Coach, but they just kept hassling me about the passes, the incompletes. So I didn't say anything.

This cop comes up to me and asks me my name. I tell him. And it's all quiet.

"I'm sorry," I say to the cop.

He touches my shoulder, not all tough or anything. Just touches it.

"All right," he says. "Let's just go talk about it, all right?"

They lead me outside with all those kids all looking at me. I don't even see them anymore. Not Ash, not Morrigan, not the guy holding Morrigan up. No one.

The cops take me to a cop car. There's three cars altogether. I'm a wanted man.

I look up the street. There's an ambulance up there, and they're wheeling that Arab kid on a bed to the ambulance.

I hurt him bad. Real bad. On the field it's fair play. Out here . . .

"You want to talk to us?" this cop goes.

"Yeah," I say. "Okay. Am I under arrest?"

"Not just yet," he says. "You still wanna talk to us?"

"Yeah. Okay."

Other cops, they start clearing out the house. Kids all over the lawn and sidewalk. Some go to their cars, a lot sit down on the grass. I'm not a football star anymore. Just a star. Some of the cops start talking to kids and I see a bunch dumping out beer onto the grass.

"Tell us what happened," this cop says. "You called nine-one-one yourself?"

"Yeah," I say, still looking at the Arab guy.

"What happened, why'd you hit him?"

"He called me names."

"Yeah? So he started something with you?"

"Kinda," I say. "But I started it first."

"How'd you start it?"

"Called him a towelhead."

The cop doesn't say anything for a sec. The paramedics almost got the kid to the ambulance.

"You're Anthony Lincoln?" the cop says, like he don't believe it. "You play for Santa Barbara High?"

"Yeah."

"I remember watching your brother play with my boy," he say. "He was magic."

"He can't play anymore. They cut off his legs." I don't think I ever said it like that. Just stated it. Goddam.

"Oh . . ." The cop scratches the back of his head. "Listen, you still got a whole other year to go in school, right?"

"Yeah."

"Do you understand that what you're describing here so far sounds an awful lot like a hate crime, and that could make things a lot worse for you?"

"I got nothing to hide." The kid is at the ambulance. "Can I talk to him?"

"Uh, not right now," the cop says. "Why don't you tell me—"

I *run*.

They can't stop me. It's like I'm on the field again, taking that ball all the way to the end zone. The cops shout at me to stop but I don't, no way, not for them. I gotta do this.

I shoulder my way between two paramedics and lean over the Arab kid.

"I'm sorry," I say, looking into his eyes. His face is busted up bad. Real bad. He only has one good eye to look at me with.

"I'm real sorry, okay, man? I didn't mean to do it, I'm sorry."

Hands grab me from behind, but I shrug them off. It'll take more than one cop to drag me outta here.

The kid's face is all swollen up. But he sorta grins, like one piece of his mouth turns up at the corner. His lips are busted and he can't talk right. Because of me. He's trying to say something.

"I'll make it right," I say, just as a bunch of cops grab me and pull me away. The cops walk me back to the squad car, and they're yelling at me but I don't know what they're saying.

"He's gonna be okay, right?" I say to them. "He's gonna be okay?"

"He'll live," one of the cops says as some other one pulls my arms behind my back. Handcuffs are cold on my wrists.

"You have the right to remain silent," this cop goes, and I tune him out. I seen enough on TV. I know my rights.

"Wait!" I hear Ashley shout.

The cops turn and kinda get in front of me, their hands out to stop her. She runs right into them like Red Rover sent her over. Like we used to play when we were all in grade school. So long ago.

"Antho!"

"S'all right," I say. "It's my bad."

"I'll call James!" she shouts. "He'll take care of it!"

"Naw, Ash," I say. "I got it, s'cool."

"Antho . . ."

"I got it, Ash. I can take it."

"You want me to call Mike?"

"No," I say. "No, I'll do it, don't say anything, okay?"

"Miss, you need to move along," this cop says, pointing back toward the yard. I can see that dude still hanging onto Morrigan, who's looking around all dazed.

Ashley scowls at the cop but backs off. "You sure?" she calls to me.

One of the cops puts his hand on my head to make sure I don't bump it going into the cop car. "I'm sure," I call back, and then I'm in the car and the door gets shut.

There ain't *no* room back here. I move to sit back against the door so I can kinda stretch my legs out. And it smells like ass, like the bathroom but worse. Like crime.

You done good, Antho.

Naw, man, I think.

You gonna make it right.

Yeah, I think. I will. Don't know how exactly. Hate crime? Black kid beatin' on an Arab kid. That's like news and shit. I was on TV once, after a game. That was cool. Next time won't be that cool.

Wait and see, little bro. Wait and see. Play it cool.

Cool? I think.

I got your back. It might not be so bad.

I hope so, bro.

I can see out the windshield that the Arab kid is talking to a cop. Probably telling him how bad I need to go to prison. That I don't deserve to play ball ever again. That maybe someone should cut my legs off too for what I did.

Goddam, Mike.

BECKETT MORRIGAN
TOMMY BRENT DANIEL
AZIZE RYAN ANTHONY
JOSH MAX ASHLEY

FUCKING BITCH!

I run to the Blazer, jump in, crank the engine, and tear down Beachfront. A flash of black and silver catches my eye to the right and I don't care, I just have to GO.

Oh, *god*. I'm gonna be sick.

Ha! "God." Right.

You hear me talking, Big Shooter? Huh? Dear Jesus: Thank you for so completely and totally fucking up my whole life, love, Josh.

Morrigan, you BITCH.

How could you do this to me, God? How? You tell me.

What did I do that was so awful, huh? I was trying to do the right thing, do what you said, and this is what I get?

Well, you know what? Piss. Off.

Hear me? PISS OFF!

I turn on my stereo. Loud. Mike Ness is singing. He has bad, bad luck.

No fucking shit! Tell me about it.

Thirteen's my lucky number, he says. *To you it means stay inside.*

I try to turn it off with my fist. The volume knob pops off, my knuckles burn bloody, but the music keeps playing.

I've definitely messed up my hand. Hey, that's what I get, huh, God? That's what I get for taking your GODDAM NAME IN VAIN.

I jerk the wheel to take a corner. Too fast. The tires skid, but I maintain control. The Blazer shudders underneath me. Reminds me of being in the tailgunner seat with Morrigan, making *her* shudder, and—

Ryan.

Ry-o.

Best buddy, old chum, old pal. What the hell are you doing to me? Like it wasn't bad enough, you just couldn't keep it in your pants, could you? God. FUCK.

BITCH!

Just trying to do the right thing, God, just trying to get it right, do what you said. Thought you'd pay me back a little there, Big Guy. Someday. It would be worth it, just like I told Morrigan.

Guess not, huh? No. Guess not.

What did I do?

TELL ME!

Go on! Let's hear it, let's hear my . . . what do you call it . . . the LITANY of my SINS. Go ahead, I'm ready. Because clearly I did something wrong. FUCKING CUSSING? Tell me. I'm all ears, God. You just lay it on. Ha! Go ahead, it's the only *laying* I'll be doing, right? Huh? Yeah.

I can't get the picture out of my head. Ryan, naked, Morrigan, reaching.

Fuck you, cocksmoker. Fuck both of you. You moved in on my girl.

Sorry. EX-GIRLFRIEND, right? Right.

The song ends, and the Dropkick Murphys comes on. Al Barr tells me that *somewhere it all went wrong, and your plan just fell apart.*

You think?

My phone rings. I ignore it till it stops, then turn the power off. I don't care who it is, I don't want to talk to them. Period.

Little help here, God? No? Didn't think so. Thanks for nothing, buddy. THANK YOU FOR FUCKING NOTHING.

Oh, sorry. Did I offend you, Big Guy?

"Fuuuuuuuuuuuuuuuuuuuuuuuuuuuuuuuuuuuuuuuuuuck!"

Good, okay, now my fingers are fucked up and my throat's sore along with them. Awesome. This is some night, yes sir, some night, all right.

I'm just going to go ahead and smoke now, Jesus. Why not? Long, slow death. Oh, yeah. Nice and slow, plenty of time to

NOT have sex. No sir, not me. I'm better than them. That's what this is about, isn't it? I am better than they are, and I guess that's my big old sin, isn't it?

How could you let her do this to me, man? Please tell me. I'm sorry if I pissed you off, I'm sorry if you're mad at me, just tell me, why did you do this to me? Why did you let Ryan move in on her like that?

It's not fair.

There, I said it. You heard me. It's not fair, and you know it. So why?

WHY?

"God, *please*..." It comes out before I can stop it.

Oh, whatever, you nancy. *He's* not listening, *he* doesn't care. If he cared, he wouldn't have done this.

"Why...?"

Shut up! Who knows, who cares. It's over. Done, dead, deceased. Get over it.

Find someone else. This summer, next year, whenever. Find someone else and go to town. *Shag* her, baby, yeah.

I love her, and—

So what. It doesn't matter. If this is love, no thanks. I'm out.

Ryan, you bastard. How could you do this? All these years and you just piss on it. Great job, my friend. I should fucking end you.

So what do you want me to do, God? Forgive her? Is that my Big Lesson? Because I'm pretty sure that is *not* going to happen. Not now, not ever. Why should I?

Why should I.

It hurts.

This whole night, it hurts. My chest hurts, God. Hey, how about a nice heart attack, just for good measure? Wouldn't that be just hysterical? HAHAHAHA!

Yeah, ha-ha.

Biggest party of the year, and this is how it ends. Swell.

It doesn't matter, nothing matters.

Nothing. I tried, and I failed. Wait, no. No I didn't. I did what you said to do, to wait. I didn't do anything wrong!

"YOU HEAR ME?!"

"I!

"DID!

"NOTHING!

"WRO—"

I take a sharp turn. Too fast. Gravel crunches and spurts under the tires. The Blazer shudders again and throws me against the door. Fishtailing now, sliding an arc back and forth across some street I don't even know. I slam the brakes. Wrong choice. Don't slam the brakes during a fishtail, that's the rule.

Yield sign. White and red, like Morrigan's shoes, leaping in front of me.

I jerk the wheel again, every muscle locked in place.

Three tons of Chevy versus three pounds of street sign.

I win. The sign flies through the night air and ends up on the opposite corner of the street. The Blazer screeches to a halt, straddling the corner curb. Thank God it's so late. No oncoming traffic.

Red lights, blue lights, a spotlight in my rearview mirror.

I lose.

Now I am FUBAR, fucked up beyond all recognition.

Song changes. Rancid. *Good morning heartache, you're like an old friend.*

God, why not just kill me now, huh? Just end the damn movie of my life, roll credits.

WHAT DO YOU WANT FROM ME?

I sit with my hands on the top of the steering wheel, breathing hard, blood dripping from my knuckles. The cop walks up slow behind me, one hand near his weapon, the other shining a flashlight into the car, probing.

I roll down the window.

"How's it going?" he asks.

There is still dust settling in front of my headlights. Correction, head*light*. The Yield sign took prisoners. That'll cost me.

"Pretty crappy," I say. My voice is shot from screaming. I shut off the engine. Rancid shuts up.

"I was thinking the same thing," he says. "License, insurance, registration."

"It's in the glove box."

"Go ahead."

I take my time leaning over, hoping he at least notices I'm wearing my seatbelt. I don't recall putting it on. I hand him everything in a jumbled pile. My hands aren't even shaking. The worst night of my entire life is only getting started, what's to be nervous about? Mostly I want sleep, or death, or for Morrigan to choke on her own drunk puke while she sucks off my best friend.

GO TO HELL, Morrigan.

"Got any weapons in there, knives, guns, rocket launchers?"

"No, nothing."

"Been drinking tonight?"

"Actually, no."

"Actually? You mean you usually do?"

Ha-ha, you got me, Ossifer. You should take your act on the road, you bastard.

"Actually, no," I repeat.

Go ahead, take me in. Reckless endangerment, destruction of civic property, speeding. What else? Let's go, rack them up. My life's over anyway.

"All right, you sit tight right here. Keep your hands on the wheel."

"Yes, sir."

He goes back to his car and calls in my information. I don't care. All I can see is Morrigan. And Ryan. If I'd walked in a couple minutes later, she'd have been riding him like a Harley.

The cop comes back in a few minutes.

"Your name sounds familiar," the cop says.

"I'm probably wanted in fifty states or something."

"I'm not that lucky," the cop says, and hands my papers and license back. "Joshua Conroy . . . you go to Santa Barbara High?"

"Yeah."

"You know a girl there named Ashley Dixon?"

Jesus, what are you doing to me? What is this? What the hell else did you have planned for me tonight, huh?

"Yes," I say, gritting my teeth.

"You Morrigan's boyfriend?"

I have now entered . . . the Twilight Zone.

"Was."

"Ah. Let me guess, something happen with her at that party by Shoreline tonight?"

"Could say that." And . . . wait, how's he know about the party? Something must've gone down.

"Ashley ever happen to mention having an older brother?"

Yeah, Morry told me, and Ash talks about him all the time. James Dixon. Santa Barbara cop. Kicked some dude's ass once a few years ago when the dude grabbed Ashley's . . .

I swallow hard. "Yeah. Um . . . yeah. Hi. Nice to meet ya."

"Well, *that* I sincerely doubt."

He's kind of grinning at me. Laugh it up, cop. Go ahead. Make my day.

"You sure you haven't been drinking tonight, Joshua? I hear some crazy stuff went down at that party."

"No, sir." Crazy stuff? If you call your sister's best friend whacking off my buddy crazy, then yeah.

"You mind if I do a quick Breathalyzer?"

"Why not."

"Okay, c'mon out here and just kick back against the truck for me, okay?"

"Yes, sir."

I do as he says while he gets his little machine. He gives me instructions, and I blow. Isn't that the truth? I blow.

I *suck.*

"Good," he says, and pulls the plastic mouthpiece out of my mouth. He checks the results. "You're ten points over the legal limit."

I almost puke. Knees turn to water. It's a lie and there's nothing I can do about—

"Just kidding!" He laughs. "Sorry, couldn't help it. You're clean. But see? Your night coulda been a lot worse, huh?"

If it was one of the guys in my place, I'd be laughing my ass off. Why can't this sort of thing happen to, oh, pick a name at random . . . *Ryan Assfuck Brunner?*

"So now the question remains, what're we gonna do about that?" He points to the Yield sign, which has cleared two lanes of street and lies faceup on the opposite sidewalk.

"Just lock me up," I say. "Throw away the key, whatever."

"Wow, you definitely had some girl issues tonight," he says. "But I understand. Morrigan's a, uh . . . unique personality."

I manage a sick smile. "True that."

"All right, Joshua," he says, "here's what we're going to do. I'm going to report that you lost control of the vehicle due to gravel on the road. So I'm going to write this up as an accident report, which you'll need to report to your insurance, and they'll pay for the damages. Probably. The damage isn't too bad, so it won't cost too much, but it might kick the crap out of your insurance for a year or two. Depends on your company."

Great. Dad'll freak.

"But you won't have to do driving school or pay a fine," he finishes. "Plus your insurance would probably go up if I did that anyway. Fair?"

"Fair," I say. "Thanks."

"And I want that headlight fixed first thing. Don't let me catch you driving tomorrow night with one headlight."

"Okay." And what else, Ossifer Dixon? Let's go, get it over with.

"And don't go bragging to all your buddies about this, or I'll come to your house and arrest you for all sorts of stuff you never even heard of. Get me?"

"You mean . . ."

"Go home, Joshua. And slow down."

"But the—"

"Go. Home."

Thank you, God. For real. Sincerely.

THANK YOU.

Maybe you do care after all. My bad. Sad that getting off with an accident report is the best thing to happen to me all week, but still . . . thanks.

"Yes, sir," I say, and climb into the truck with my accident report.

He gives me a nod, gets in his cruiser, and drives away.

I pull off the curb and turn left as headlights light me up again. I pull off to the side of the road to calm down before I try driving home.

So that was close. And it could've been worse.

Yeah. Worse.

The car passes me—going the speed limit—then hits the brakes.

NOW WHAT?

The little blue car swings around and comes up behind me. They park the car, and the headlights shut off. I wonder for just a second if it's like gangbangers or something. Of course, right *after* a cop leaves. But the people who get out of the car are anything but.

I close my eyes and rest my head on the steering wheel.

Un. Be. Fucking. Lievable.

I get out of the Blazer again as Morrigan's parents jog up to me; Mr. Lewis looks pissed, Mrs. Lewis looks pissed *and* worried.

Hey, God, remember when I asked you what I did to deserve this? I renew the question.

"Have you seen Morrigan?" Jim Lewis demands.

No *Hi, howareya, how'sitgoin'?*

"Yes," I say, and kick back against the truck as Mrs. Lewis joins him.

"Where is she?" she asks.

I shrug. "Partying. Getting hammered."

Zing! Take that, bitch. Explain that to Mommy and Daddy!

Mr. Lewis fumes. Good.

"We broke up last week, you know," I add. "I know she told you, Ashley said so, so why ask *me* where she is?"

They stare at me dumbly. Unreal. They have no idea what I'm talking about.

"Do you not hear a word she says to you?" I ask them.

"We thought everything was okay," Mrs. Lewis says.

"Well, it's not!" I say. "Do you want to know why she broke up with me? I'll tell you. It's because I *wouldn't* sleep with her."

Aw, yeah. Couldn't have said anything better. They look *slapped*. Chalk one up for the ex.

"That's right!" I say, because this feels *good*. "I would *not* have sex with your little girl, and she broke up with me because of it. That's the kind of *adorable little princess* you've raised. And if you don't believe me, you can ask her yourself!"

Mr. Lewis recovers from the smackdown and puffs out his chest, all manly. "Don't you dare talk about my daughter that way, you little shit!" he roars at me and takes a menacing step toward me.

Oh, bring it on, old man.

Bring that shit on.

Tie my ass into a pretzel or send me to the ER, whatever, do your worst, because frankly, I've had it with sitting on my ass and I got nothing left to lose.

But Mrs. Lewis grabs his arm. "Jim," she says. "Hold on."

He hesitates.

Lucky thing. I'd've drop-kicked that sucker.

Mrs. Lewis pulls him back so *she* can take a step toward me. "Are you being straight with us, Josh?" she asks. Lines crease her forehead. I've never seen her this worried.

"You think I could make something like that up?" I say. "It's the truth. And if you want to kick my ass for being honest with you, then step on up, because I'm done being a nice guy about it."

Am I really picking a fight with my ex's parents? On the street?

You're damn skippy I am.

Mr. Lewis still looks pissed, but he doesn't make a move. I hate to say, I don't think it's because I intimidated him. Damn.

Mrs. Lewis looks back at him, then again to me.

"What else?"

"What else, *what?*"

"What else do you . . . know about her?"

I lift my arms. "I have no idea what you are asking."

"Is she . . . all right?"

"All right?" I spit back. "I don't know. Why are you asking me? *You're* her parents."

Mrs. Lewis looks back at her husband again, and they stare at each other. What the hell is *this?* It's like they're using telepathy or something. Fucking parents, man.

"Do you know where this party is?" Mr. Lewis says finally.

I shrug. "Near Shoreline Park."

"We were headed that way," he says.

"Then you're headed right."

"Was Ashley taking care of her?" Mrs. Lewis asks.

"I don't know. Most likely. I didn't really talk to either of them. Morrigan's not my girlfriend anymore, remember? So, to be perfectly honest, not my problem."

"You're right," Mrs. Lewis says, which shocks the hell out of me. "It's not your problem. I appreciate your honesty."

She goes back toward the car, squeezing Mr. Lewis's hand as she passes him. "Let's go home and wait for her."

"What?" he shouts. "After driving around all night looking for her!"

"Jim," Mrs. Lewis says. "Please. If she's with Ashley, she'll be fine. Ashley won't let anything happen to her." She glances at me. "Was Ashley drinking?"

I'd love to lie, just to make this harder on them and by proxy on Morrigan, but I can't quite pull it off. "No," I say. "She was just keeping an eye on Morry. She's sober."

"See?" she says to Mr. Lewis. "Let's go." She walks around my truck and I hear her get back into the Civic.

Mr. Lewis turns his gaze on me. He walks up and crosses his arms.

"So you didn't sleep with her?"

I look that sucker right in the eye. "No."

"I'm just supposed to believe that? Pretty girl, couple teenagers out all night at a party?"

"I don't much care what you believe, man. It's the truth. Ask her yourself. I made a promise, and I'm keeping it. Not for nothing, man, but even if she came crawling back to me right this second, I still wouldn't do it. But I'm sick of trying to explain why to everyone, so you're just gonna have to deal."

He arches an eyebrow, and holy *shit* does he look like Morrigan right then. Crazy.

"I find out you're lying," he says, "we're gonna have a talk."

I lift my arms again and take a step back. Kicking range, just in case. "We're having a talk right now, man. I mean, you make it sound like we *should* have done it. And if that's the case, you got major problems that got nothing to do with me."

His chest swells up and I brace for a swing. Oh, do it. Do it, and put an end to this glorious goddam night, man.

But Mrs. Lewis calls from the car. "Jim, come on. We should get home."

He glares at me for another second, then pivots away and stalks back to the car.

"And hey, one more thing," I call. "You don't have to tell me how pretty your daughter is. I know that. Why don't you tell her for a change?"

It's one of the things Morrigan's told me over the last couple months, that this dickwad hardly even looks at her. If that's true, and it is based on what I've seen at her house, then he deserves to hear it for squaring off with me.

I swing back to the Blazer and climb in, happy to have the last word.

I pull out onto the road. I can see Mrs. Lewis on her cell in my rearview mirror. I hope she's able to get Morry on the phone again. That would be priceless.

I drive slow the whole way home just in case another cop's on the prowl. It's been the worst night of my life, but I'm also the luckiest son of a bitch I've ever known, and I don't want to press my luck.

So, hey, God. What's up, how's it going?

Heh.

Are you mad?

Mom and Dad are going to be pissed, you know. You *do*

know this, right? You know that even though I got a lucky break, they're still going to string me up by my balls, as Morrigan would say.

Morrigan.

Morry.

My girl.

God? Listen, man . . . I'm sorry. I am. I'm not even sure for what just yet, but I am.

I miss her. And I'll do anything to get her back. Anything.

"What?" I say out loud, like I can't believe myself, and I sort of can't.

Get her *back*? On what planet is that even *remotely* sane? She made herself perfectly clear, last week and tonight, at the party and in that bedroom with one of my best friends.

Still. I miss her. And if there's anything I can do to get her back, then . . . *by God* . . . I'll do it.

But not if it means sleeping with her. I can't go back on that. Not even for her. Not even for you, God. That's right. It's not about you anymore. At least not right now. If I sleep with her now, then all I'm doing is hurting her. I won't do that.

Not that that's going to happen. It's too late to even think about it. Man, I am so stupid.

I get home in one piece and go up to my room without waking up Mom and Dad. They knew I'd be out late anyway. I sit at my desk and stare at nothing, then try to get my mind off Morrigan by playing Spider Solitaire. But I can't sleep, I can't stop thinking. I pull out my phone and stare at *it* for some time instead.

"You sure about this?" I say to myself.

No. Never have been. But I have to try it.

She'll be asleep, I tell myself. It's so late—correction, early—and she'll just be passed out anyway.

Maybe that's better. I can leave a message. Yes, leave a message, shoot the ball into her court, let her figure out what to do with it.

Yes.

I have to try.

If Tommy or Matt or Daniel or Ry—

If one of my *friends* was here, he'd try to stop me. He'd tell me it was a bad idea. He'd prob'ly be right.

I flip open my phone and turn it back on. It warms up, then shows I have a message and have missed three calls.

All of them from Ryan.

Huh.

I punch in my voicemail and listen.

"Josh, man, it's Ryan. Look, you have to understand, nothing happened, okay, man? I swear to god, man, nothing happened. She came in right after Bethany left to go get me a beer and like attacked me, I swear I wasn't going to do anything with her. All right? Man . . . call me back, okay? Let me know you got this. I swear to you, Josh, it was not what it looked like, I wouldn't do that to you, okay? I swear, man. It's a total misunderstanding, that's all I'm saying. Okay? Okay, call me back. Later."

I close my phone.

Ryan is many things. He's a man-whore, screwing anything

that breathes, but he's never moved on anyone we were dating. Or ex-dating. Never. He's also not a liar. He hates it when people are pissed at him. He wouldn't risk it.

I should have known that. Should have stayed and talked to him, asked him what happened.

That doesn't excuse Morrigan, though. No fucking way. Right?

I mean, even if she was drunk and so pissed off she couldn't see straight . . . that's no excuse. And she did already break up with me. It wouldn't have been cheating, technically.

Right?

I don't know, God. I don't know.

I just need to hear her say it one more time. Just say . . . "It's over." Once more, to be totally sure, then I'll leave it alone.

Okay? Just let me at least try. And if she says Over, then she says Over, and I won't blame you anymore. But if you could just do this one thing for me, man, just this one time . . .

I open my phone again and hit my contact list. Her number is right at the top as always on my Contacts.

1-Morrigan. I press send. And wait as her phone rings.

Pick up, Morry. God, just let her pick up.

BECKETT MORRIGAN
TOMMY BRENT DANIEL
AZIZE RYAN ANTHONY
JOSH **MAX** ASHLEY

A COUPLE COPS ARE TALKIN' TO THIS HUGE BLACK GUY, ANTHONY. He plays football and whatever, I remember talkin' to him when I tried out a couple years ago. Pretty cool dude. I was surprised he got up in that Arab kid's face like that. Maybe it was the alcohol.

From where I'm standin' on the front lawn, I can see the ambulance parked several yards up the street. The medics are rollin' a bed uphill toward the van. I catch a glimpse of the guy on the bed, and man, he is messed *up*. Looks like he's been hit by a bulldozer. I just met him tonight. Not a bad guy. He's gonna be a senior next year. He says he's friends with Beckett, that he was gonna find a way to get her to come talk to me.

So much for that. She never even showed. Brent was right, I guess. How stupid am I? Wasted three years, pinned it all on the night *after* we graduated, how the hell did I think I was gonna see her again?

The cops are still talkin' to Anthony, but I'm too far away to hear. Man, I tried to break that up! They squared off and I stopped it, I thought. Shit. It's my fault.

Except I *did* break it up, and that dude—Azize?—left the house. Anthony musta followed him out after I went back to the kitchen for a beer.

There're three cop cars altogether, but I'm not sure how many cops. About a hundred, it feels like. They keep movin' around and they all look alike, so it's too hard to count 'em. A few of 'em are keepin' an eye on groups of kids who are sittin' on the curb or front lawn.

A cop asks me a couple questions, but since he's askin' if I saw anything happen *outside,* I don't tell him about what Anthony and Azize said to each other inside. None of my business. The cop goes on to some of the more drunk-lookin' kids. I keep an eye out for Brent. Lost track of him a while ago, and he has our boards.

One minute we were hangin' out in the backyard, right after I tried to break up Anthony and Azize. The next, a buncha kids jumped over the wall and took off while the rest of us froze when a cop started shinin' his flashlight in everyone's faces. I lost Brent after that. Maybe he jumped the wall, too.

I didn't see Beckett Montgomery anywhere. Man.

One lucky dude, that Azize guy who got beat up. I mean, as

far as luck goes. Coulda been worse, based on Anthony's size. I move over to the edge of the lawn where the grass meets the sidewalk for a better look at what they're gonna do to our all-star receiver.

Ashley Dixon runs over toward Anthony, but the cops stop her. She shouts his name. Anthony waves her off, like she don't need to get involved. She talks to Anthony for a sec before the cops holding her back make her step off. Ashley goes back over to this dude Ryan, who's holding her friend Morrigan up under the arms, and he passes her over to Ashley.

"What's going on?"

I turn to the quiet voice I hear on my left.

Beckett Montgomery.

—is looking up into my face, scared and confused and worried all at once.

Beckett Montgomery, still wearing her Rasta hat and a beautiful long skirt and kick-ass shirt, and oh god, *it's Beckett Montgomery talking to me.*

"Beckett," I say before I can stop to think to say anything else.

Beckett blinks at me. "You know me?" she says, her voice still quiet, and her voice . . . I want to taste it on my tongue, it's soft and scratchy and a little deeper than I woulda expected. And sexy as hell even though I'm sure she don't mean it to be.

"Yeah," I say, and want to punch myself in the dick for being so stupid and not sayin' somethin' cool.

We just stand there and look at each other for about ten

years. The streetlight near the house where the party is—*was*—is falling right across her eyes, these green, green eyes that look like a cat's but so much more like elegant and wonderful.

I'm gonna pass out or something.

"Have . . . we met?" Beckett asks.

"N-no," I say. "N-not really. Uh. I just. I've, um. Seen you around."

At least I don't tell her I stalked her for three years. Dumb dick.

Beckett nods a little, then looks over at the ambulance.

"So, what's with . . . ?" Beckett says.

"Oh, um . . . this one dude beat up this other dude," I say. "That one Arab kid."

She whirls around on me. *"Azize?"*

"Think so."

"Who beat him up?" she demands.

I just point. Anthony Lincoln is talkin' to some cops, and Beckett looks all confused.

"*Antho* hurt him? Anthony Lincoln *hurt* Azize?"

"I—I think so . . ."

Beckett takes off toward the ambulance, and I follow. She might need me. Or somethin'.

They've got Azize propped up on the bed, and have cleaned him up a little. He's startin' to swell up some, but with the blood washed off he don't look as bad as a few minutes ago. A cop is next to the bed, so Beckett stops short, and I almost run into her. I kinda wish I would've. To be *so* close, you know? But she's really freakin' about Azize, so I'm glad I didn't run into her.

"So you're saying you just wanted to wrestle him?" the cop says, and he don't believe it for a second. "You were both just, uh, horsing around?"

"Yes," Azize says.

"He threaten you, son? Tell you not to talk to us?"

"No, sir."

"Did he call you any names or anything while you were, uh, playing? Some witnesses have stated there were, uh, racial epithets being shouted earlier?"

"No, nothing like that. Just teasing things."

"You're sure about that?"

"Yes, sir."

The cop nods, kinda like to himself, then says, "Well, you need to go get checked out. We might have some more questions for you later, all right?"

"Yes, sir."

The cop walks away toward the other cops and Anthony. Beckett waits till the cop passes us, then rushes over to Azize, her hands on the bed's rails. I take a couple steps, but don't get too close. The paramedics are gettin' ready to start loadin' him into the ambulance.

"Azize!"

Azize holds up a hand to stop the medics. He smiles, and it's kinda gross, 'cause his face is so busted up.

"Beckett."

"What happened, are you all right?"

"I'm fine, Beckett. Really."

"What did he do to you?"

"It was just playing around. It got out of hand is all."

"Azize, that's not playing around! I know Anthony, I need to know what happened, who started it?"

Azize smiles again a bit. "It's not important."

"It is to me. Please."

"Beckett," Azize goes, all quiet like, and he lifts her hand off the bed, takes it in his, and I get so *jealous*. "Please believe me. I was afraid and angry. And when people are afraid and angry, they do stupid things. It's no problem."

"Miss, we really need to get him outta here," the paramedic goes, and Beckett takes a step back.

Azize turns his head a little toward my direction, wincin' like it hurts to move. His good eye opens a bit wider for a sec, then he gets that messed-up smile on his face again.

"Have a good night, my friend," he says.

I sorta wave a little, feelin' like an asshole. Guess when it's all said and done, he did bring us together after all. Now it's up to me to do somethin' with it.

They load him into the ambulance as Beckett glances at me.

"Everything is all right!" Azize says to her just as the doors close. She don't see him gimme a thumbs-up, like secretly.

Beckett turns back toward the house. The cop who talked to Azize is off to one side with another cop.

"So, you're friends with Azize?" I say.

Beckett don't look at me. "Yeah. No. Sorta. We traded

comics in the library once in a while. He likes the Hulk." *Now* she turns to me. "Do you know what happened?"

"Dunno. It was like racial or something."

Beckett sorta scowls and I feel like I did something wrong. "Racial how?"

I really don't know how to handle this so she won't get mad at me. "Well, like, maybe Anthony said some shit? Um, said some *stuff,* and Azize said some stuff back. I dunno."

"What did Anthony say?"

I clear my throat. This ain't the conversation I rehearsed for three years.

"You sure you wanna know? 'Cause if you're friends with both of—"

"Yes. Tell me."

So I tell her exactly how it went down in the house between 'em. "And Azize left, I watched him go. I dunno what happened after that."

"God," Beckett whispers. "It must be his brother."

"Huh?"

"Anthony's brother. Mike. He's stationed overseas."

"You mean like in the Army?"

"Yeah. In the . . . Middle East."

Oh, *shit.*

"Oh," I say, 'cause I really don't know what else to say. "That's messed up."

"But Azize is from Turkey," Beckett says. "He's not even . . ." She stops and rubs her eyes. "Whatever," she mumbles. "Stupid night anyway."

I can't take my eyes off her. It's here. This moment, this stupid moment I should have and could have created any time I wanted the past three years and now it's here and I dunno what to do with it after all this noise. Plus she's lookin' at the cop car Anthony's in now, like I ain't even here.

Perfect. Just perfect, you know?

Then someone's sayin' her name.

We both turn. Two girls are walkin' toward us, Ashley Dixon and Morrigan Lewis. Ryan's off by himself, talkin' on a cell.

Morrigan looks like she can barely walk, let alone talk. She's hangin' on to Ashley's arm for dear life, draggin' her red Converse on the lawn. Ashley, on the other hand, looks stone-cold sober. Designated driver, I guess.

Ashley scowls at me, but only for a second. "Hey, Max," she says, like all kinda cautious.

"Hey," I say, and can't stop my eyes from darting to Beckett, who's got her head tilted down like she don't want to be recognized. I hope Ashley don't wanna start anything with me 'cause I turned her down that once. It ain't that she ain't cute or nothin', she's just not . . .

"Beckett?" Ashley says. "You're still here. I thought you left."

"Yeah," Beckett says back to Ashley, brushing a stray hair out of her face. I don't actually see the hair, though. It's like she's imagining it. "I, um . . . was on my way home."

Ashley peers at Beckett like she's searchin' for something. "You picked a hell of a night to try partying."

Beckett nods, says nothin'.

Ashley frowns. What's up with these chicks, man? And why won't Ashley just *go*? Obviously she's not too pissed at me for not goin' out with her, so that's something, but—*leave*, woman!

"You hear what happened?" Ashley goes.

Beckett nods.

"It's so weird," Ashley says. "I wouldn't've thought Antho could do something like that."

"He was drinkin'," I say. "Polished off a bottle of Jack, I think."

"Jack . . . ?" Ashley goes, then like grits her teeth or something, glancin' at Morrigan. "I swear," Ashley says, real quiet. She looks at Beckett again. "You going to talk to him? To Antho?"

Beckett don't say anything, just jerks her shoulders real quick. Ashley frowns again, then takes a big breath and tries to pull a smile on.

"So! How's your mom? You took off so quick back there earlier, and I feel like I haven't talked to you in forever . . ."

To me it looks like she's just tryin' to find somethin' to say. And what's this *earlier* shit? Beckett was here the whole time?

But something happens then. Like an electric current passes from Beckett to Ashley and back again.

And the next thing I know, Beckett Montgomery grabs my hand and is squeezin' it so tight that I almost yell. I manage to keep it under control as my heart, which was already double-timing it since Beckett started talkin' to me, switches over to a fast punk beat.

Oi oi fuckin' oi!

"She," Beckett says, still squeezin' my hand, but she don't say nothin' else.

Ashley looks from her to me, and back again.

Beckett is noddin' her head, little jerks back and forth, her eyes roamin' all over the yard and, I'm pretty sure, not seeing anything.

"She, um," Beckett says at last, and right then, Morrigan interrupts with this huge puke that barely misses her shoes. Nasty. Me and Beckett take a step back at the same time.

"Oh, god," Ashley says with a sigh. "Third time's a charm. I think that's our cue. Sorry."

"It's okay," Beckett says quietly, and to me, looks relieved. My fingers are startin' to go numb from her grip. Like I care!

Morrigan Lewis wipes her mouth and grins like an idiot, then offers this little gem: "My mom fuckin' sucks."

"Morry," Ashley barks, and Morrigan laughs, damn near spillin' them both to the lawn. "Beck, I'm sorry, she's—"

"It's okay," Beckett says. "No big."

"Look," Ashley says as Morrigan starts turning as green as the grass, "we'll hang out, okay? Would you? To see if there's anything we can do to help Antho out? I'm going to talk to James, but . . . Antho's going to need friends. Are you in?"

I see Beckett swallow hard and press her lips together. "Maybe," she whispers.

"You still have the same apartment and phone number and everything?"

"Yeah, um . . . yeah."

"Okay. Listen, I'll call you tomorrow afternoon or something, okay?"

Beckett nods. "Sure. Okay." She brushes again at that invisible hair on her face. "Unless, you know . . . I mean, if you don't, it's okay."

"No, no," Ashley says. "I will. Look, I gotta get Morrigan home." Ashley stands there for another second, though. "Beck . . ."

"You should go," Beckett says. "Get her home safe."

"Okay," Ashley says. "So . . . see ya."

Beckett says the same to her, and Ashley half carries Morrigan over to a beige sedan, keepin' an eye on Anthony the whole time, who's outta the cop car now. That's weird. Thought they'd've carted him off to lockup by now. Anthony is standin' up, arms still folded, noddin' his head at whatever the cops are sayin' to him. Ashley shoves Morrigan into the passenger seat, gives one last look at Anthony, another back at me and Beckett, then gets in her car.

Beckett turns to me, then looks down at our hands. She lets go, and it hurts. Not my hand, but like . . . my chest. Like it's empty.

"Oh," she says. "Sorry, I didn't mean—"

"Naw, it's no problem, I—"

"—I wasn't thinking, I just—"

"—didn't bother me at all, no—"

We both stop, realizing what a couple of dumbasses we sound like. I do, anyway.

"Thanks," Beckett says, and kinda taps my arm. I swear to God it tingles when our skin touches. 'I guess the party's over, huh?"

Or maybe it's just startin', I think, but I'm not quite dumb enough to say it.

"Guess so," I say, and my triple-time heartbeat somehow manages to speed up even more.

"Listen," I say. "Um, I was, uh . . ."

And I got nothin'.

Not a word, not a clue. I draw the biggest blank ever known to mankind. It's like that moment on a half-pipe when you've gone way too high and even though your neck is probably gonna break in the next second, that moment catching air is both the most, like, exhilarating and most terrifying, and it lasts for-fucking-ever.

Beckett looks up at me, all like curious. "What?"

She is the most beautiful woman I have ever seen.

"D'you . . . have a . . . minute?"

"Um . . ." She glances at Anthony, still surrounded by cops, but not in cuffs anymore. "Sure. I guess."

I look around. The party is definitely breakin' up. Cars are being started and driven away. Ashley's tryin' to pull out, but people keep cuttin' her off. Cops are still watchin' bottles get emptied and instructing sober kids to drive, but the crowd is only about half what it was a few minutes ago.

I point up the street, where it's a little more secluded. "You mind if we go sit over there for a minute?"

Beckett looks to where I'm pointing. "I guess."

We walk past the house, up the street, and sit down on the curb about ten yards from the nearest car.

This is it. That moment after you launch, hanging in midair, wonderin' if this time you pushed it too far and the pipe is gonna break your spine, but part of you don't care because you can fly.

The moment I've been plotting and planning and rehearsing for three years.

I'm sittin' next to Beckett Montgomery.

And I still got nothing to say. Nothin' that tastes right. Not after the fight, not after Ashley pokin' her nose in.

Beckett folds her arms on top of her knees and rests her cheek on her arms, lookin' at me. How cute is that?

"So what's up?" she goes.

I take a deep breath.

"So, um," I start, "I think I had biology with you sophomore year."

Beckett stares at me, like she's really studyin' what I just said. "Yeah?"

"Uh-huh. And, um . . ."

"You *remember* me from sophomore year?"

"Um. Well. Yeah. Your freshman, my sophomore, I mean."

"Well," she says with this little laugh. Then she goes, "I don't remember ever talking to you before."

"Yeah, well. Um. You always looked like you needed to be someplace, so."

Beckett turns away, so her chin's on her arms, givin' me her profile. "I did," she mutters.

"I signed your yearbook once." Dude, really? Is that all I can come up with?

I see her blink real quick, like she's surprised. "Yeah?"

"Once, yeah."

"What did you say? 'Have a cool summer'?"

I rub the back of my head, stallin' for time. Is there a right answer to this? I don't fucking know! What I know is what I wrote: *Your awesome see u next year.* I didn't sign my name.

"Um . . . somethin' like that. Stupid, huh?"

"No. If it was from the heart, I'll take it."

It was. God, it was.

Beckett laughs suddenly, burying her face in the basket of her arms. I try hard to see through her skull and find the joke. Is she laughin' at me? Of course she is. *Duh, I signed your yearbook, duh!* God, I suck.

But her laugh . . . the first time I've ever heard it, and it makes me feel . . . so . . . *happy.*

"What?"

Beckett lifts her head. "I ran away from home once. I went all the way down to the corner of the street, you know? Which is like Africa when you're five."

I sort of chuckle, but it sounds all wrong and I choke on it. "Yeah," I say, and wish like hell for a glass of water. And for her to laugh again. To hold my hand again.

"You want to know something?" She don't look at me.

"Sure."

"No one came to get me."

Not sure where to take that, so I come up with the brilliant response of "Huh?"

"When I like 'ran away,' " she says. "No one ever came out to get me. I think that's why I did it. Just to see."

You are a weird, weird chick, I think. *And I'd give anything, anything in this world to make you feel better. Or kiss you.*

Beckett sighs, and for one second, I'm sure she's heard my thoughts. She's gonna get right the hell up and call me a prick and take off. I wouldn't blame her.

"Sometimes you run away from home not because you're going any further than the corner, but because you want to see who will come running after you," Beckett says.

I relax a little. She ain't psychic, thank god, and I try to listen close as she goes on.

"You know it's like immature, but this is the only way to be sure," Beckett says. "But sometimes, the sun really does set, and you're still there by the stop sign, waiting. That peanut butter sandwich you packed for the trip is long gone, and you're hungry. But no one has come to see if you're coming home or not. It's like they figure you'll either really take off, or you'll come crawling back. Either way it's not their problem."

Beckett pauses, and flings a pebble across the street. Then she looks into my face, and she is somehow becoming more beautiful by the second. How is that even possible?

"You're still the jackass for sitting at the corner in the dark," she says, and laughs again, but not like it's funny. "You know why I came here tonight?"

"To party?" I say, but it don't sound right.

"To see if anyone would talk to me," Beckett says. "I thought I was invisible. I wanted to see if anyone ever . . . noticed me. I kinda keep to myself."

"You're not invisible," I say. Are you kidding me? *Invisible?*

Beckett looks into my eyes. "Did you know who I was when you signed my yearbook?"

"Yeah. I did."

"Were you stalking me?" She bumps her knee against mine and *fuck* I wish I was wearin' shorts, to have that much less clothing between her skin and mine, I don't care if it's her knee or her foot or anything, just so long as it's her.

"Maybe a little," I say, tryin' to sound casual and *not* like a stalker. "I mean, not like, in a creepy way. He said hopefully."

Beckett grins, just a little. "No worries."

Tell her now. Tell her.

I take a breath, ready to spill my guts. Ready to hand her my heart and let her kick it right over a cliff.

She meets my eyes again and gives me a slight smile. A fireworks factory goes off in my stomach, fucking KA-BLAM!

"Thanks for talking to me," she says.

"Um. Sure."

And then.

Beckett Montgomery.

Leans over.

And hugs me.

My body goes numb and I can't hug her back. Did *not* expect this. My nerve endings are like short-circuited, electrifying my scalp and the hairs on my arms. Her cheek is pressed into mine, and it's like . . . like raw silk, which I felt once when my mom was sewing some kind of pillowcase or something, the softest, smoothest texture you can ever imagine.

I just landed that air on the half-pipe.

Beckett gets to her feet. I just sit there like a jackass before I can shake myself awake and get up.

"I'm Max," I say, 'cause I dunno what the hell *else* to say.

"Beckett," she says. "Nice to meet you, finally." One corner of her mouth turns up in this adorable smile.

I know your name, I hear myself thinking. *I know, I know.* Then: *She's getting away, man. Ask her, ask her, ASK HER OUT!* I scream inside my skull. *Dammit, dammit, dammit, why did you come here tonight and talk to her if you weren't gonna even ask her out? Get her* number *at least.*

I want to hold her hand again, gently this time, but I'm too scared, so I shove my hands into my pockets so I won't try.

I feel something in my right pocket. A card.

My Lucky 13! card.

I pull the card out of my pocket, flipping it over in my fingers like I'm gonna do a magic trick with it.

Hey. Maybe I am.

I swing my arm out toward Beckett, offering it. "Here."

Beckett takes the card and studies it. "Coffee Cat? That place rocks. I'm thinking of getting a job there this summer. Um . . . you know all the numbers are punched?"

"Yeah, I know. Sorry about that."

"What am I supposed to do with this?" She's sorta smiling when she says it.

"It's . . . a good-luck charm," I say.

"Really?"

"I hope so," I say.

Beckett gives me a bigger smile, lighting her face up in the darkness. I realize it's the first time I've ever seen her smile that big.

"Cool. Thanks. You know thirteen's not a lucky number, right?"

I look into her eyes, which are shining under the moon-light.

"Yeah," I say. "I've heard that."

I feel myself grin like an idiot just as Brent's voice sounds from up the street.

"Max!"

I turn automatically. Brent's standin' on the sidewalk in front of the house where the party has officially broken up, holdin' our boards, one in each hand. He lifts his arms in a giant shrug, like, *What the hell you doin'?*

I don't know! I want to yell at him. I truly don't. I wave at him to hang on for a sec and turn back to Beckett just as a car rolls to a stop nearby.

"So, um . . . maybe I'll see you around then?" I ask, tryin' not to sound too hopeful.

Beckett folds her arms and lifts her shoulders up, like she's cold or something.

She doesn't say a word.

BECKETT MORRIGAN
TOMMY BRENT DANIEL
AZIZE RYAN ANTHONY
JOSH   MAX **ASHLEY**

I GOT MORRIGAN INTO THE CAR WITHOUT ANY MORE VOMIT, THANK GOD. By the time I pulled the seatbelt across her, she actually looked better. My guess was she got the worst of it out of her system.

"Blegh," Morrigan said.

"You can say that again," I told her.

"Blegh," Morrigan said.

"Right," I said, and shut the door.

I walked around to the other side of the car, but stopped as I saw Beckett a little ways up the street talking to that guy Max. Amazing. I've never seen her talk to *anyone* since freshman year. I'd asked Max out once before, but he'd declined. He was nice about it, though.

I got in the car and started the engine. Morrigan held up a hand and said, "Wait."

Morrigan opened her mouth, and I thought, *Oh, god, not in the car, please not in my dad's car.* It's not that Dad would be mad, but I'd be the one to clean it up.

Morrigan let out this raw, juicy belch that curdled her lips and looked like it probably tasted as bad as it sounded.

She dropped her hand with a content sigh. "Okay," she said. "Carry on."

"Dork," I said, and started rolling down the street. "You sobered up now?"

"Sadly, I think so. Blegh."

I was going very slowly, as people from the party were all evacuating to their various cars. People turned in front of me with their vehicles or stumbled across the street. I noticed Ryan Brunner off to one side of the front yard talking into his cell phone, and making pleading gestures to absolutely no one. Talking to Josh, I guessed. I hoped they worked everything out; it was a hell of a dumb way to lose a friend. And Ryan'd been very nice tonight, all things considered.

Because of all the foot traffic and people trying to drive away at once, it made getting down the street something of a chore. I didn't mind. It gave me time to watch Beckett and Max.

I was pretty disappointed the night turned out the way it had. This whole thing with Antho and that kid Azize, that was messed up. Anthony had always been a great guy. Then Morrigan and her—what do you call it—*attempted dalliance* with Ryan . . . that must've sent poor Josh screaming for cover. I hoped she'd explain it to him, regardless of their dating status.

But really, most of all, I was disappointed because Beckett had shown up to the party out of nowhere, and I had barely said ten words to her, after all this time. That sucked. And I hated that I'd yelled at her earlier, even if she did seem to have forgotten or forgiven me by the time I walked up to her and Max on the sidewalk. I didn't mean to yell at her on the patio; it was just so frustrating having her stand there not looking at me, not talking to me, like she'd rather be anywhere else in the world.

Of course, my dearest best girl Morrigan might've had a little to do with that. *Girls,* honestly.

I was glad to see Beck at least talking to someone. And I meant it when I said I'd call her. Maybe she'd even answer this time. I knew her mom's number was in the phone book, which I'd have to look up since my phone was out of commission. Despite her refusal to call me back, I hadn't ever deleted her number. I can be too optimistic for my own good sometimes.

Hell with it, I thought. I'm going to make sure she knows I'm serious about talking again. Whether she wants to or not. Plus who knew what kind of trouble Antho was in, and he might need our help. She couldn't turn her back on *him,* too. At least, I didn't think so.

I stopped the car opposite her and Max and rolled the window down.

"So, um . . . maybe I'll see you around?" Max was saying.

He looked so hopeful it was almost mythically tragic. I honestly expected Beck to blow him off. She'd do it nicely, but she'd do it. She'd done it to me and Antho. But anyone who could help Morrigan to her feet after the way she'd behaved toward Beckett wasn't someone who could be the bitch Morrigan accused her of.

"Okay," Beckett said, and I thought, Here it comes. Brace yourself, dude.

"Would you . . . call me?" Beckett asked.

Max looked exactly as shocked as I felt. He recovered quickly.

"Yeah, yeah, sure, absolutely," he said. "Um. Yeah!"

"Okay. Maybe we can do coffee."

"Yeah, sure, perfect! Um . . . when's good?"

"I don't know—tomorrow night?"

I felt myself nod. Yes! Tomorrow night! Good job, Beck.

"Tomorrow night, yeah," Max said. "That'll work. Cool. Oh, um—I guess I need your number."

Beckett gave it to him, and Max punched it into his phone.

"All right," he said, and smiled. I remembered then why I'd asked him out—he was nice, and he was *hot*. Instead I ended up with the catastrophe that was Todd. Well, that wasn't Max's fault.

"Awesome," he said. "I mean, cool. All right. Cool. I'll talk to you tomorrow, then. Beckett." He said her name like an afterthought, like he was trying it out.

"Cool. See ya, Max."

I wouldn't have thought his smile could get any bigger, but it did. Max nodded once, big-time triumphant, then ran full steam back up the sidewalk to the house where the party had been. I watched in the mirrors as he took a skateboard from his friend Brent, dropped the board to the ground, and skated into the darkness. He popped an awesome ollie on his way. I wondered if he ever surfed.

"Well," I said out the window, and let it come out a little *saucy*, "looks like everyone's having quite a night."

Beckett jumped, like I'd startled her. She blushed and hugged her bag to her chest.

"Oh, hey," she said, and watched Max disappear down the street.

"Listen, you need a ride or something?" I said. "I got to take Morry home anyway. It wouldn't be a problem." Not a problem because I assumed Morrigan was already passed out. She was never that quiet for that long otherwise.

Beckett studied me for a second, then turned some sort of business card over in her fingers. It was shiny on both sides and caught the light from a streetlamp. Finally she hustled over to the car and got into the backseat.

"Thanks," she said quietly.

"No problem," I said, and waited again as another car pulled in front of me.

Morrigan sat up and looked over her shoulder at Beck. Still awake after all.

"Oh," she said. "Hey."